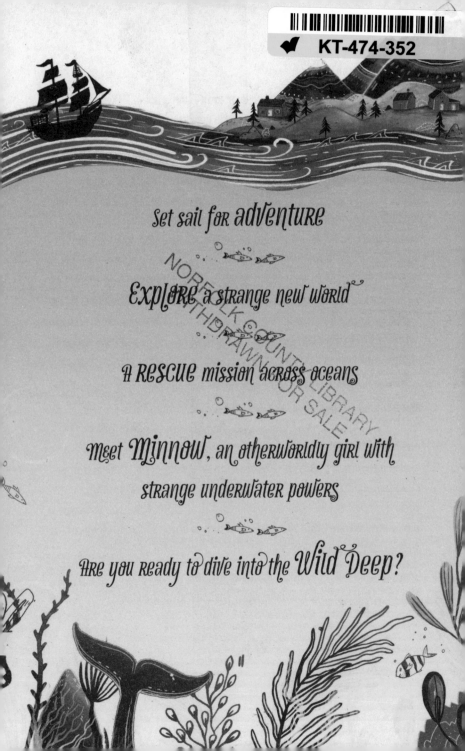

Set sail for adventure

Explore a strange new world

A RESCUE mission across oceans

Meet Minnow, an otherworldly girl with strange underwater powers

Are you ready to dive into the Wild Deep?

A note from the author,

When I was very little, maybe three or four, I had a hook. Not a pirate's hook. It was more like a crooked plastic claw that could open and close to pick things up. Some doctors had decided that the hook would help me to do things, as I only had one hand. They were wrong. The hook made everything harder. One day at playschool we were all playing a game of Peter Pan. I desperately wanted to be Wendy; she was floaty and kind and had an acorn/kiss necklace. But someone else had already been chosen to be Wendy. So I asked if I could be Tinkerbell. She was small, flighty, and jealous, but she could fly and glow like a star. But someone else had already decided to be Tinkerbell. So who could I be? There was a moment of hesitation where the word seemed to hang in the air. Somehow I felt it being spoken before it was even said, like the opposite of an echo. 'You can be Hook.' Shame crept over me, my cheeks turned red, and I ran away. I didn't want to be a beardy man with a pointed hat and a fear of crocodiles. I wanted to be someone wonderful.

Soon after, I hit my dad in the eye with the hook, then I bashed a hole right through a door, and that was the end of it. But I never forgot the moment of being likened to a villainous male pirate. There were no fearsome women pirates for me to fall in love with, no fabulous heroines brandishing hooks. Though the stories I knew were full of girls who looked similar to me—Alice, Goldilocks, the children from The Faraway Tree—there were none who had one hand, or a will so defiant they could break out of a closed door.

Many years later, I became a mama to my own wilful child, Amelie: a beautiful little girl of dual heritage. I rushed out to the shops

to find her books with children in them who looked just like her. But there weren't enough. And really this was why I became a writer. I had always had stories unspooling in my heart, but now I had a focus and a burning reason to write. For every child needs mermaids or pirates or princesses in their own image, to brighten their imagination and put them in the heart of the story.

When Amelie was five or six we went to the fifth birthday party of a curious little girl who liked many interesting things, including sharks. In the party bag, to our absolute delight, we discovered real miniature shark's teeth. Amelie just so happened to have lost the tooth in the corner of her top jaw. 'Look, Mama. I'm a shark!' she cried, holding up the tooth, which fit like magic into her mouth. My heart almost stopped, and in that moment I saw them: a bright-eyed, brown-skinned girl with shark's teeth, and a pirate mother navigating a sea of dark storms and strange magic. I knew I had to find them. To write them into a story. And so, the Wild Deep came to be and Minnow arrived with her not quite bones, and her silvery scars, and her shark's teeth.

I hope you will enjoy reading this story as much as I have enjoyed writing it. It's a complete work of fiction, but there is a tiny silver thread of our family woven all the way through. And if, like me, you believe in the possibility of mermaids, you will know that parts of it are very, very real. Like Minnow's grandmother says in the book, 'There have always been Mer. They have swum through every time and culture and have as many names as the night.'

Cerrie Burnell

For my beloved Amelie,
And all those who dream of The Wild Deep

OXFORD
UNIVERSITY PRESS

Great Clarendon Street, Oxford OX2 6DP

Oxford University Press is a department of the University of Oxford.
It furthers the University's objective of excellence in research, scholarship,
and education by publishing worldwide. Oxford is a registered trade mark
of Oxford University Press in the UK and in certain other countries

British Library Cataloguing in Publication Data

Data available

ISBN: 978-01-9276754-7

1 3 5 7 9 10 8 6 4 2

Printed in Great Britain

Paper used in the production of this book is a natural,
recyclable product made from wood grown in sustainable forests.
The manufacturing process conforms to the environmental
regulations of the country of origin.

CERRIE BURNELL

The Girl with the Shark's Teeth

OXFORD

UNIVERSITY PRESS

Chapter One

THE MOONLIT MAP

Minnow lay just beneath the surface, still as driftwood, counting the seconds as she held her breath. Her heart thudded in her ears, fierce as thunder, and she balled her fists to stop herself moving. The still waters of Brighton marina weren't ideal for hiding in, but at least the dark would help her keep out of sight. Minnow loved the silver-dark of a starry sea, where she could dive through the waves unhindered. Or the night horizon beyond the twinkly pier, where the indigo tides felt like freedom. Even the evening marina was cool and familiar to her. But the far down, deep, dark made Minnow fearful. That place in seemingly bottomless oceans where the light is lost and the water swirls like inky gloom. It was that thick, breathless dark Minnow dreaded: the dark where the beast lived. The beast was a silent watery creature that swam through Minnow's dreams. Many times Minnow woke gasping for air. Then Mercy, her mother, would pull Minnow into her arms and sing a sea lullaby to soothe her.

With the slightest flick of her ankle she curved down around the draft of the boat that was her home: *The Seafarer*. Minnow had taught herself to slow-drift in a circular motion, barely sinking or rising, so she could move underwater almost unnoticed. All around her the underside of other boats hung in stillness, but *The Seafarer* cast a deeper presence, as if it was cut from the very bones of the sea. It wasn't *The Seafarer's* size that set it apart, but its aura: a work of sea-bound fiction imagined with wood. A beautiful mermaid figurehead carved from black timber peered out from its prow, her braided hair sculpted to look as though it was flying out behind her.

Minnow flattened herself against the side of her boat and gazed up, hoping that anyone who caught sight of her would put it down to a trick of the moon. Suddenly there was a splash, as something wolf-shaped dived from *The Seafarer's* black deck, and Minnow smiled. A wet nose dipped down and two sapphire-blue eyes sought out her own. Minnow reached up and hugged Miyuki her beloved husky, lightly tapping the dog's nose to signal silence. Then, using Miyuki's silvery body to shield her, Minnow slowly stood. Her toes recoiled as she slid her red Salt-water sandals into the oozing silt at the bottom of the marina and peeked her head above the waterline, her eyes darting anxiously to *The Seafarer*'s deck.

There was her mama, Mercy; hair the colour of blood. She was wearing jeans, cowboy boots, and a flowing silken shirt. *Fighting clothes*, thought Minnow darkly. But instead of unleashing the wrath of a thousand furies upon the three strangers—men who had just stepped onto her boat—Mercy instead struck a match on the heel of her boot and lit a cigarette. Minnow in all her twelve years had never seen her mama smoke, and as she watched her now Minnow had the shivering feeling that she was staring at a stranger.

The three men watched in tense silence, as Mercy sprang onto the neighbouring boat *The Water Lily*, and with the edge of her hook cut a sprig of fresh mint from the deckside herb garden. She stamped her cigarette out on *The Water Lily*'s deck, shoved the mint into her mouth, swung her legs easily onto the promenade, and sauntered away. Minnow felt a scream begin to rise up in her throat. What was her mama doing? Abandoning *The Seafarer*, disrespecting their neighbour's boat, and acting as if Minnow and Miyuki didn't exist. Minnow stood to her full height, head and shoulders out of the water now, spinning in the silt to go after her mum. But one of the men suddenly moved across *The Seafarer*'s deck, shining a torch into the water, and Minnow instinctively shot back below, pulling Miyuki with her, thankful that the rich golden-brown colour of her skin made it easier to blend into the night water.

The Seafarer swayed and moaned as the men's heavy footsteps moved up and down, echoing out through its draft, as if the boat had a heartbeat. Minnow edged closer and tried to catch a sense of the conversation up on deck. One voice was low and rough, and another sounded loud and boastful. The third—the man who, moments before, had tried to warn Mercy—was whistling a tune.

Minnow scrunched her eyes shut and tried to follow the sound. Something about the whistled tune felt comforting. And then she almost opened her mouth to gasp—it was her lullaby! The song which could carry her straight back to childhood. To the safe embrace of her mama's arms, the diamond-sharp edge of Mercy's hook glinting in the starlight. Red hair streaming in the wind as she sang. It was the song to hush nightmares, banish the beast and the dark ocean. How did this whistling stranger know her song?

Moving away from the boat Minnow sank down, clutching *The Seafarer'*s rusted anchor, and settled cross-legged amongst the reeds and silt. In the watery dark she ran over everything that had happened in the last five minutes and tried to make sense of the unfolding strangeness.

It had been a perfectly lovely Brighton evening. Starlings cut across the sunset, newly awakened stars twinkled on the water, and a wild wind danced with the rigging. Minnow had slipped into a deep sleep in the green, silken hammock, her legs gently twitching, unable to keep still. Miyuki sat proudly beside her as usual, quietly keeping watch while Mercy was out, teaching her evening yoga class.

Minnow had been dreaming of the deep ocean when her mama suddenly swam into her dream. *Amelie*, she called in a voice of ice and salt water. It was only ever her mum who called her by her true name, and only when something was *seriously* wrong.

Minnow's eyes fluttered open. Her head was still foggy from the medicine her mum gave her sometimes to help her sleep, but she'd pushed through the tiredness and made herself sit up. A streak of scarlet caught Minnow's eye across the harbour.

Mercy was running towards her with the urgency of a breaking storm. Minnow sat up straighter, her heart quickening. Something was wrong. Could her mum have woken her with a thought? It wasn't entirely impossible. Mercy had found Minnow in dreams before, but this felt different. As Minnow watched, her mum shimmied up the mast of an empty boat and then with a motion that was part falling, part flying, she dived from sail to sail, landing on *The Seafarer* as though from the sky.

Even from a distance Mercy looked unmistakably like a pirate. It was the gleeful gleam of her ruby hair, a red that rivalled sunsets. And her eyes, such a pale shade of blue they made people think of the Arctic. And her teeth, of course. A mouth that glistened with silver. And her laugh. Minnow had witnessed the power of her mama's laugh many times. A laugh that made married women want to abandon their husbands and run away to sea. And caused grown men to forget their own names. And inspired children to live a life of adventures. But really it was her hook that clinched it.

Anyone could have a heart-stealing laugh and six silver teeth. But on the end of Mercy's right arm was a curl of fairy-tale silver, slim like the sliver of a new moon, its point encrusted with diamonds. It wasn't particularly frightening, but it was—as Minnow knew—deadly sharp. The hook was real, but a costume too. A clever way to make holidaymakers believe that *The Seafarer* was a real pirate ship, so they would pay a small donation to look around this floating museum of marvels. And Mercy and Minnow could afford to live.

Using the hook's half-moon curve, Mercy slid down the rigging, seized her daughter's hand and Miyuki's collar, and yanked them both behind a huge black sail.

'I need you to hide,' Mercy hissed. Minnow blinked in confusion. Was this some bizarre game? It certainly didn't feel like one; it felt like the air was being squeezed out of her lungs and the world was sliding away from her.

'Hide?' Minnow mumbled.

Mercy nodded, her blue eyes worryingly bright. 'Go below. Wait till I'm off the boat, and then watch for the pier lights to go out. Soon as it's dark sail to Grandma's.'

'Sail to Reykjavik—?' Minnow started, but Mercy clapped a hand over her daughter's mouth and stared at her with a look that could knock eagles from the sky. Minnow was deeply unnerved, her feet aching to run.

And that was when she had first seen the lone figure heading towards their ship.

He was tall, almost willowy, and even though he was hurrying there was a calmness to him. As he stepped into the moonlight Minnow saw that he had beautiful black skin, and a veil of long, neat dreadlocks hanging over his face, masking his features. He climbed onto the boat with the gentle ease of someone who knew *The Seafarer*, though Minnow couldn't remember ever seeing him before.

'Mercy!' His voice was low and pleading.

'Wait here,' hissed Mercy in Minnow's ear. She nodded and held her breath as Mercy slipped out from behind the sail and swept across the deck. Minnow felt the night crackle with electricity, like the moment before a firework is lit. Would there be a terrible row, a dreadful fight? Would her mama brandish her hook? Minnow clenched her fists, her heart roaring. But none of those things happened. Instead Mercy and the stranger stopped inches away from each other, his head slightly bowed, her face tilted towards the stars so they must have been staring into each other's eyes.

'I found you in time,' said the tall stranger, a smile finding its way into his voice. 'You've got to go. Jah Jah's not far behind me—'

Mercy tossed her flame-coloured hair. 'Let him come.'

Delicately, the stranger took hold of Mercy's face in his hands. 'It's serious this time. Jah Jah's got a new business partner, Louis, who's got a fibreglass cage and a harpoon . . . The man can dive as deep as Jah Jah and he wants to catch a mermaid for his daughter.'

Mercy laughed, but the sound sent a chill creeping through Minnow's soul. 'I can't run Ely, if Jah Jah finds me again . . . it's too dangerous.'

The man slowly folded his arms and gave a slow, sad nod. 'Is she here?'

Mercy shook her head. 'She's with her grandma for the summer.' And Minnow suddenly realized they were talking about her. *Why?* she thought crossly. What did this Ely know about her?

He drew a long breath. 'You know I can't stop Jah Jah, Mercy, you know I've tried. If you want to save the ship you must move away from here and hide the map.'

Mercy nodded then she rose onto her toes and very lightly kissed him. The wind held its breath. Minnow was speechless! Her mum normally fought with men, hurled them overboard or beat them at cards, not kissed them . . . Mercy hurried into the galley, then reappeared holding something that faintly glimmered. Ely stared at her a long moment, then turned reluctantly away and moved back onto the promenade, hiding himself in the shadows.

Mercy ducked behind the sail and pushed a rolled-up piece of parchment into Minnow's hand. It was smooth, and cool to the touch, and seemed very faintly to sparkle. There was a flash of diamonds and a cutting of metal as Mercy removed the silver locket that hung round her neck and pushed it into her daughter's hands. A whirl of anxiety danced through Minnow's bones. This was her mum's beloved locket that she wore at her throat every day. Why was she giving it to her?

A thousand questions burned on Minnow's lips, but there was no time to ask, for into the lamplight stepped the other two men—Jah Jah and Louis. The first was also tall but fast-moving with purpose. His black skin glistened as if he'd come from the sea and his hair was a mass of thick, twining dreadlocks, which reminded Minnow of the roots of a great tree. Though he was dressed in the casual clothes of a surfer, a clump of golden rings glittered on his fingers, and his watch, Minnow knew, was one of the best you could buy to go diving with.

The second man had white skin that was deeply tanned and weathered from years of being outside. His blond hair was scrunched back in a rough ponytail and he moved with the easy confidence of someone who had grown up on boats. Trailing behind them both, drifting with the sadness of a ghost, came Ely.

As the men stepped onto *The Seafarer*, Mercy raised Minnow's chin with the point of her hook. 'I love you my darling,' she whispered, her voice brittle as salt crystals.

Then Minnow had felt herself being tipped overboard, lifted by the soles of her feet, the way they had rehearsed out deep when they were diving. 'You never know when we might have to abandon ship,' Mercy used to say when Minnow was a child. But Mercy was a sailor of extraordinary skill. She could stare into the heart of any hurricane and defy it with a riotously mocking smile. Throughout a childhood of high waves and sea storms Minnow never had 'abandoned ship'. At least not until this moment. A moment later Miyuki had followed her into the water, then Mercy had strolled away into the moonlight leaving the boat in the hands of the three shadowy men.

Above her, torchlight slanted through the water and Minnow risked moving to the surface to take a breath. An echo of conversation floated down. 'It's not here;

she's taken it with her.'

'Are you sure, mate? There are about a thousand maps on this boat.'

'Not like this. It's like it's made from moonlight.'

Minnow remembered the strange parchment her mum had given her. In a clean, agile glide she moved to the other side of the marina where a wall separated the boats from the sea. In the shadow of the wall Minnow raised her lips to the surface, like a whale taking air. Then she settled back on the marina's muddy bed and pulled the parchment from her back pocket, blinking with delight as it unfurled in her hands, showing itself indeed to be a map. A map the colour of moon dust, or silverbirch bark, waterproof under the sea. *This must be the map they are looking for.*

Tucking it back into her pocket, Minnow rose to the surface. *The Seafarer* rocked almost violently as the three men climbed onto the walkway, and started heading towards town. She couldn't let them get away. She had to know what was going on. But the harbour was full of tourists and she knew she mustn't be spotted emerging from the water, late at night. She cast about and noticed a flock of starlings settled in sleep on the sails of a small boat called the *Louisa-Mae*. Darting over to it, Minnow gave the little white hull a push and smiled as the tiny birds burst into a whirlwind of wings. As a light cheer went up from the crowd, Minnow shot out of the water in a single ceaseless motion, her sandals hardly brushing the wooden planks of the boardwalk, as she dashed into the bushes unseen.

In the water Minnow was graceful but on land it was a different matter. With a wild stumble she lost her footing and fell, grazing both her knees and kicking up salt dust. Sea lavender prickled her skin and she squeezed water from her braided hair, counting a full minute, allowing her heart rate to pick back up and her lungs to adjust to breathing freely again. Slowly she stood up, a trickle of blood running down her leg and disappearing into the flowerbed. Great—another scar. Minnow was covered in them. Most were temporary, fading away like the moon at dawn, but others stayed, marking her brown skin with trails of silver. None were quite as vivid as the two symmetrical scars that glimmered on either side of her neck. They were blossom-pale and completely identical, and though Mercy had told Minnow they were birthmarks, Minnow had never seen another birthmark quite like them.

Minnow took a deep breath, turned away from her home and walked in her dripping wet shorts and t-shirt up onto the main walkway, whistling for Miyuki as she went. With a bound of salt water her dog was at her side and moving in time with her past the overcrowded restaurants.

Tourists gave them bemused looks, but Minnow

pretended not to see them. What did they know about living by the sea?

'I think someone's fallen in,' said a jolly dad with sunburnt cheeks. Minnow looked him straight in the eye the way she had often seen her mother do.

'Nope,' she said with a grin. 'Just been feeding the walrus.' And with no further explanation she began to run. Not fast at first, just a jog to get away from the flocking crowds, and then she was flying down the concrete steps, racing after the three strange men. What had Mercy said? *Wait till the lights on the pier go out, then sail to Grandma's.* Well Minnow wasn't waiting for any such thing.

Running on land did not come naturally to Minnow. In fact, up until Minnow was five, no one had known if she would walk at all: it was as though she could not bear her feet to touch the ground—her legs seemed unable to hold her. She had tried with crutches, but that only lasted six days before one was lost over the side of the pier. Then Mercy had bought a bright red wagon—a Radio Flyer—which a young Miyuki eagerly pulled. It was one of the reasons Mercy had chosen a sled dog, easily capable of towing a child. Then Minnow startled everyone by clambering out of the Radio Flyer one day and grabbing the dog by the ears. At first, she was dragged, then she started skidding, and then soon she was galloping. Minnow literally ran before she could crawl. Her consultant, Doctor Stephen, was particularly astonished, being sure that Minnow's skeleton didn't have the right density to support her weight. Mercy had rolled her eyes and touched his hand in a way that made him blush. She refused any more X-rays of Minnow and instead presented Doctor Stephen with a bottle of vintage port. The two had remained friends ever since, and any further medical advice was given over dinners on *The Seafarer*. Minnow was still clumsy on land, but her lungs were strong from free diving and her stamina was unending.

Ahead of her, Minnow spotted the three men closing in on Mercy. Shock rattled through her and Minnow's body was caught off balance, so she was forced to launch herself over the side of the seafront and onto the stony beach. She knelt up, blinking in surprise as she saw her mum do the unthinkable: board a coastal bus to town. Mercy didn't own a car—she would sooner surf on the rooftop of a train than ride in one, and she certainly never bothered with the bus. If Minnow and Mercy left the city they did so by boat. Mercy was only content by the sea, its unpredictable nature matching her own and answering her wildness. But now here she was on the bus the same as everyone else. Minnow watched with a chilling curiosity as the three shadows slunk onto the same bus before it closed its doors and moved away.

Miyuki pushed her wet nose into Minnow's shoulder

and she clambered unsteadily off the beach, following the bus route as it wove along the coast. Mercy gave no sign of noticing her pursuers as the bus stopped and she sauntered off, heading through Kemptown towards the Gala Bingo hall with the relaxed ease of a local, the men following in her wake.

Minnow's head was humming with confusion. This had to be the strangest behaviour she'd ever witnessed from her mum and that was saying something. Then it hit her like the crack of a thunderbolt. Mercy was heading towards a long-deserted train tunnel. 'Oh no,' breathed Minnow desperately. Her mum was leading the men to their death. That's what would happen; Mercy would kill them in the dark, dank tunnel. 'Oh Mama,' Minnow gasped, suddenly feeling an overwhelming sadness for the unsuspecting intruders. For a moment she considered sprinting to the police station; it was near enough, but what would she say? 'My mum is about to murder three strangers in a tunnel!' They would think her crazy.

With shaking hands she pulled a bandana from her pocket, threaded it through Miyuki's collar and tied her loosely to the lamp post. 'Stay,' Minnow murmured, kissing her dog's snowy forehead. On trembling legs she crossed the road, dropped to her hands and knees and followed the men inside the tunnel.

Chapter Two

THE MERMAID
SCALE PENDANT

A dank stench of tree roots and thick-spread moss coated the air like a fog. Sweat ran off Minnow's skin. This was the kind of darkness she dreaded. But the tunnel was so humid and earthy, so different from the lightless ocean in her dreams that soon her fear cooled and Minnow inched forwards. The men were gathered in a small group up ahead, and they were arguing, their heads bent together like drooping flowers.

Minnow had never been good at keeping still. She'd never been able to sit at a desk for long before the urge to run took over. Even now her ankles were quietly trembling. She ground her teeth in concentration, tasting the metallic tang that came from having four silver teeth, a bit like her mama. Another little mystery about herself she didn't quite understand. She had tried asking Mercy about her teeth, but she never got a straight answer.

Jah Jah seemed to be losing patience. His movements were so sudden and clipped with fury he reminded Minnow of a warrior. 'We set this place on fire we'll find her much quicker,' he growled.

Minnow hoped with all of her bones he wasn't serious. Then Ely spoke up. 'You need to show some respect. She'll come when she's ready.'

As Minnow's eyes became accustomed to the dark, she noticed Jah Jah was wearing a seashell-shaped pendant, which emitted a low eerie light. It was one of the loveliest things Minnow had ever seen, both smooth and rough, like the inside of an oyster shell or the scale of a fish. In the pendant's pale luminescence Minnow caught sight of a familiar silhouette: a woman with wild hair and a hook pressed against the wall, just behind the men. The shadow-form of her mama reached for something, clasping her hip on impulse. Minnow drew a sharp breath. She knew this movement; Mercy was checking for her dagger. *It's just part of her pirate costume though. She would never actually use it*, Minnow told herself, willing the words to be true.

In a lightning-fast movement which only Minnow saw, Mercy pulled her phone from the turtle-hide bag across her shoulder and dropped it on the ground, quietly driving the heel of her boot into the screen, so it splintered. And then she advanced upon the men.

'So my sweet, we meet again,' she chuckled, moving towards Ely as if the meeting upon *The Seafarer* had never happened. Before he could reply, Louis barrelled into Mercy, knocking her to the ground. Minnow gritted her teeth, ready for what would come. Mercy sprang to her feet, hook poised like a blade, spinning between the three men, a whirlwind of scarlet and silver. There was a scuffle and a thud. Minnow couldn't see what was happening, but each of the men cried out in pain. Someone swiftly gasped and Minnow was shocked to see her mama lying like a fallen princess on the dank earth.

'Hey, hey careful there, Louis,' cried Ely.

'We need her alive,' Jah Jah added, handcuffing Mercy's wrist to his own and pulling her to her feet. She came up at speed, hook first, shaving away part of his beard and grazing his chin.

'Lovely to see you, Elijah,' Mercy cooed.

Elijah? Jah Jah must be a nickname, thought Minnow.

Jah Jah laughed almost fondly. 'The pleasure's all mine,' he hissed. Then Ely stepped between them, a calm hand on both of their shoulders. Though he said nothing, his presence was rooted in a posture of peace that no one seemed able to challenge.

Louis gave Mercy a sort of bow: 'G'day miss. The

name's Louis. Heard you can lead us to a mermaid.'

Minnow actually let out a sigh of dismay. So that's who these witless men were. Myth-chasers, Sea Hunters, mermaid-seekers. Fools deluded enough to believe that *The Seafarer* really was a pirate ship, and that all of its strange exhibits were relics from a long-lost ocean. Clues that led to a secret world where mermaids and marvels basked in the moonlight. It had happened before. Folk had become obsessed with the dream of finding a mythical creature and had begged Mercy for help. But all she could do was to offer them some rum and tell them a fairy tale, before sending them on their sad and sea-swept way.

Mercy tossed her head back, crimson hair whipping Jah Jah in the face. She met Louis's jovial stare with a somewhat startling smile, and Louis seeing her face properly for the first time was dumbstruck. She seemed to be looking deep into his soul and from the look on her face, it was clear that she found him lacking.

Mercy narrowed her blue eyes at him, her voice soft and menacing like a curl of smoke. 'Mermaids don't exist, my love.'

'Then how do you explain this?' spat Jah Jah, holding up the shimmering pendant. Minnow saw it wasn't quite shell-shaped but more scale-shaped, from a very large fish.

'And don't these belong to you?' chimed in Louis,

pulling a small velvet box out of his pocket and flipping it open. Minnow strained her eyes to see what was inside. It looked like six small, very sharp teeth.

They were cream in colour with the gum end stained like rust, either from age or blood. The bottom tip of each tooth was ever so slightly green, as though it had been dipped in algae. Minnow thought of her mum's wondrous smile and the six silver teeth that shone from it. And suddenly she began to feel incredibly anxious, as if she might have to bolt for fresh air. Her feet began tapping uncontrollably, rustling the dead leaves and soil on the floor.

'Those teeth are clearly from a museum or an end-of-the-pier cabaret show,' Mercy giggled, but her laughter sounded forced. Jah Jah yanked her closer to him, and quicker than lightning Mercy's hook was at his throat. Minnow nearly gave a squeak of protest. As much as she disliked this Jah Jah, she didn't want her mum to murder him over the sake of a fictional sea creature. Again Ely stepped soundlessly between them. Without speaking he unhooked the cuff on Jah Jah's wrist and fastened it carefully to his own, so he and Mercy were now bound together. Then ever so slowly he moved the diamond-sharp hook from Jah Jah's throat. Quite astonishingly Mercy let him. She didn't so much as flinch.

'If you don't mind, miss, we'll need to check your belongings,' said Louis somewhat cautiously. Jah Jah pulled the dagger from Mercy's hip then snatched her turtle-hide purse, scattering its contents onto the ground. Mercy yawned nonchanlantly as credit cards, a stick of kohl, a small knife perfectly crafted from a fish bone, a broken compass, a waxen lip palette and a family pass to Drusillas Park Zoo tumbled onto the earth. Jah Jah studied the family pass. 'What's this? You got family now?'

Mercy leaned towards him with a dreamy grin. 'Oh yeah,' she simpered, 'I've got a husband, six children, two houses, and a Mercedes.' Minnow felt her heart go still. Her mum was denying her very existence. *To protect me. So the men don't come after me,* she told herself. But it stung like the burning stroke of a jellyfish.

'There are two ways this can go,' said Louis, taking charge before another fight broke out. 'You can come peacefully. Sing your song or whatever, and show us to the mermaids. Or we'll have to take you by force, we'll ransack your boat, we'll . . . '

Mercy drew in a quick sharp breath and spat on the ground, rather close to Louis's flipflops. She met his gaze with a murderous stare, her voice low like a whisper of death. 'Whatever you wish.'

'We'll go get the car ready. Ely, follow when you hear me whistle,' ordered Jah Jah, storming off towards the tunnel entrance, Louis following close behind. Minnow managed to still her fidgeting bones as the men hurried past her, their footfall kicking up a light spray of soil which settled on her hair like dark snow. Ely bent down, noticing Mercy's phone lying in the dirt.

There was one remaining bar of battery and when he shook it, a single image flashed across the cracked screen. He squinted as if looking at a photo through shards of ice. It was a child. A child with the brightness of the sea in her smile, her tightly-plaited hair bound up in a knot. For a long moment he stood very still, gazing at the phone, and then he turned to Mercy, his brown eyes holding a question. She stared back at him, blinking slowly just once before she smiled, a terribly sad little smile that made Minnow want to cry.

A shrill whistle rang through the tunnel. Ely dropped the phone, scuffing over it with soil, before leading a silent Mercy towards the others. The only sound was the tread of their light feet and the gentle jingling of shells, which came from a bangle Ely wore of cowrie shells and bright red thread. Minnow had to bite down hard on her hair not to whimper as they passed her. Then she counted to ten, leapt up, and darted after them.

Chapter Three

THE GIRL, THE DOG, AND THE PIRATE SHIP

Outside, the night was fresh and cool. The group had crossed the road and Minnow stood in the shadow of the bus stop watching them. 'Hope you like flying, Miss Browne,' said Louis with a forced enthusiasm.

'I don't have a passport,' Mercy answered, and Minnow got the distinct impression that Mercy sounded worried all of a sudden. She couldn't remember them ever travelling anywhere except by boat.

'We're going to fly anyway,' Jah Jah barked.

Mercy glared at him hatefully. 'Yeah. How?'

'Magic,' he answered clicking his fingers. And at that moment, as if summoned by enchantment, an SUV with blacked-out windows pulled up silently in front of them and Mercy was bundled in.

'Shoreham Airport, boss?' asked the driver.

'Where else?' beamed Louis.

Minnow opened her mouth to scream, but the air dried her throat, stealing her voice like a sea-witch's shell. As the car sped away, she could do nothing but shiver in the darkness, then run to her dog and let loose her tears in Miyuki's snowy fur.

After a moment Minnow dropped her arms numbly from around Miyuki's neck. In her heart a terrible stillness seemed to keep her from breathing. She had to move, had to get back to the boat, but her legs were heavy as wood. It was the dog who nudged her into motion. Dizziness rushed over Minnow like a breaking wave. For a moment the street lights hurt her head and the warm night seemed to burn. 'Water,' Minnow spluttered, and she didn't mean to drink.

Water was the only antidote to feeling overwhelmed. Whenever her senses went into overload or the world felt too sharp, she would run for the cool of the sea. 'To the beach,' she murmured, staggering to a run, the familiar patter of Siberian paws spurring her on. The road they were on led straight to Marine Parade, which overlooked the sea. They reached it in a scattering of heartbeats, girl and dog nose to foot. All of the stairways that led down to the beach were locked at this time of night, a turquoise-blue six foot gate forbidding you to enter. Neither Miyuki nor Minnow even paused to breathe. Instead their paces quickened, matching each other perfectly, and at exactly the same moment they leaped.

The dog, whose coat was woven from winter, bounded over the gate like a silver-black wolf, landing in a streak of claws on the stairs beyond. Minnow half vaulted, half flew over the gate, banging her ankle and ending up in a diagonal crouch like a skateboarder. She lurched forwards unsteadily, half sliding, half tumbling, scalding her hands on the rusted iron banister as she tried to regain her balance, before crashing to her knees at the bottom. She was up again in an instant, barely registering the pain, just charging on towards her moon-bright sea.

Dogs weren't allowed on the beach in summer, and children weren't allowed in the sea at night, but these rules had never applied to Minnow. She fled to the sea, dipping down into the crystal coolness, relief finding her among the starry water.

Minnow knew every curl and dip and stone of the shore. The way the current could snatch at you. The rush and gasp of the tides. She was used to night dives in the shallower parts of the beach, a golden fish in midnight ink. Down she shot to the black sand, where the sea sang at its loudest.

Listening to waves was like hearing the voice of the elements, or the heart of the earth. Minnow knew this rhythm well and tonight the sea felt charged with whispers, urging her forwards. Above her, two moons shone brightly. The full summer moon, and its shimmering reflection, glittering ghostlike on the water. She tried to make a clear line of her muddled thoughts, like she did when charting a course by the stars, or learning coordinates on a map. But nothing made sense. Her mama had let the men take her away, to protect her? And now all she could do was to follow her mum's last instruction: sail to her grandmother's house. Which just so happened to be in the Icelandic capital of Reykjavik, a journey Minnow had never done alone. But there was no time or space for doubt. Surely her grandmother would know what to do?

With this thought bright in her mind Minnow arced backwards up to the surface, feeling her spine lengthen and ease into place. Her head broke the water beside Miyuki, just in time to see the lights on the pier flicker and go out. Darkness fell across the Brighton seafront and a feeling of dread gripped Minnow. They were supposed to be back on board *The Seafarer* preparing to set sail. This was her cue and she had missed it. 'Miyuki, home!' she cried, turning towards the marina and diving beneath the waves.

Minnow zipped through the water like a rocket unleashed, moving in a style that defied any stroke. It wasn't front crawl, or breaststroke, or butterfly, because she swam underwater and mostly with her back. Her arms pointed in front, her hands joined like the tip of an arrow. The speed at which she travelled was breathtaking, and yet Minnow only came up for breath twice, mostly to encourage her beloved husky. As Minnow approached *The Seafarer*, she caught sight of something sparkling beneath the waves, like the trail a jellyfish makes. She spun around in the sea several times before realizing it was coming from her back pocket: the map!

Minnow pulled herself on board the boat and studied the map more closely. She had seen a great many maps in her time, both real and fictional; maps that existed in made-up worlds, maps charting journeys that could be sailed in less than a day, and maps that told of secret waterways, shared only between true sailors. Mercy's collection was astounding. Yet this map was different.

Its touch was like kelp, rubbery cold, and it shimmered the electric blue of lightning. When Minnow held it up she saw it bore an intricate sketch of a huge swirling lake, which seemed to be in the middle of the sea. It was concave, like an upside-down iceberg, and had been loosely split into three parts: Vintertide, Darkentide, and Somertide. There was nothing to suggest whereabouts in the world this strange lake was. Its border was simply marked by shoals of different fish, a carefully drawn lighthouse on the Vintertide edge, and a looming black cave and golden shoreline close to the Somertide boundary. Its compass diagram was embossed in gold like a stamp, but it pointed south instead of north. Its meaning was way beyond Minnow, but she adored it all the same. The last thing her mama gave her, it meant everything for that reason alone.

Across the map in faded ink were drawn the words *The Wild Deep.* She almost laughed. The Wild Deep was an imaginary ocean where fables lived and breathed. Like Neverland or Narnia, you could reach it only through stories and dreams. *Those men really were fools if they thought they could enter a magical ocean.* Then a bright thought struck her. *Perhaps without this map they'll give up and let my mum go . . .*

Minnow shuddered, remembering how the men had been ruthlessly searching her home for the map. She scanned the deck for damage, but to her amazement there seemed no sign of the intruders. They had covered their tracks impeccably. *They must be proper criminals,* she thought, and her heart gave a small lurch.

Minnow inspected the galley, but again nothing seemed to have been touched. The galley's walls were still lined with coral-cut shelves crammed with bottles, and poisons, and brightly flowering plants, each exactly as it had been. A glorious secret cave of a place, warm with lantern light and the smell of sea-herbs.

With a gulp of relief Minnow placed the glowing map on the navigation table, securing it with a beautiful glass paperweight. Inside its dome a turquoise starfish was suspended in time as if it were sleeping. It was one of Mercy's favourite things. Minnow bit down hard on her plaits, trying not to think about her mama being bundled into the car. A shower of salt drops scattered against Minnow's legs as Miyuki shook herself dry. 'Hey!' Minnow squealed, grabbing an old check blanket and rubbing the dog's fur so it didn't dry salt-stiff. Miyuki gave a low whine of appreciation then started pleading hunger. Minnow swiftly filled Miyuki's bowl and turned back to study a real map—the map that would take them to Reykjavik. She didn't really need to look at it because its landmarks were like grooves upon her heart. It was the route they took every summer to get to Iceland. To Reykjavik, and to Minnow's grandmother, Arielka. The thought of that fair little city was like the beam of a lighthouse guiding Minnow to safety.

Below the galley in her mum's cabin a clock chimed quarter past midnight and Minnow forced herself into action. Hurriedly, she eased a well-fed Miyuki into her harness. Then she dropped to her knees and attached the harness to the circular pulley, or capstan, which wound in the anchor. 'Go girl,' she whispered, giving Miyuki's forehead a kiss. The dog gave a yip of a growl and bounded into motion, moving in a perfect circle, wrenching up the ancient anchor from below. Minnow leaned over the side of the boat, rounds of rope ready in her hands to bind the heavy structure in place. She'd done it before. She knew how to work every inch of this boat on her own, but Mercy was normally there to guide her. But her fingers were trembling so much that the rope wouldn't hold. She scrunched up her toes in determination and tried a different knot. Then she focused her mind on the task ahead, closing her eyes to feel the direction of the wind. Minnow placed her hands on the rigging to let out the sails; crossed amidships and gripped the wheel. She untied Miyuki and gave her a new task of being the lookout. Then, as she'd done many times before with her mum beside her, she began to steer *The Seafarer* away from her berth and into the middle of the Mainer making certain nothing stuck, or jarred. They had to go slowly, the boat was so huge, and they couldn't risk rocking anybody else's. As they inched past their quietly bobbing neighbours, both girl and dog held their breath, as if an absence of movement might make them narrower. With clenched teeth Minnow manoeuvred the boat around a massive bend, then curved sharply left—or port as Mercy called it—before gliding through the opening in the wall to meet the white waves of the sea.

A lone gull swooped down and landed on the mast of the boat, its wings the colour of stardust. It gave a long sorrowful cry, before diving away to seek out midnight fish. Minnow turned and watched as the familiar lights of the marina slowly became part of the landscape, drifting out of vision. Then the girl, the dog, and the pirate ship were alone on the water, with only the moon as their guide.

Chapter Four

A WIND OF WILD BIRDS

With the blacked-out silhouette of the pier receding behind her, Minnow tried to imagine the way her mama moved around *The Seafarer*. Mercy did everything with a fighting spirit and an angel's grace, sailing one wingbeat ahead of the wind. *I don't have wings*, thought Minnow, *but I do have an Arctic dog*. She pulled the belt from her shorts and tied the ship's wheel to a large potted citrus tree in the corner of the deck, then dashed to Miyuki's side and wound in a small sail. 'We've got to be one step ahead of the tide, three leaps ahead of the wind,' she told Miyuki, directing her to the helm. The dog took up her place with a keen eagerness, eyes bright like sapphires of the sea, tail curved in sea dog mode.

'It's just one trip,' Minnow told herself, imagining the sleepless stars that would guide her. 'Mama never studied the art of map-reading.' And she was right,

Mercy did it all by intuition, as if those tiny fragments of light in dark skies, the screeching wind, and fierce waves were woven from the same threads of the universe as her.

To get to Reykjavik Minnow would have to sail the British coastline as far as Orkney, then bear North towards Iceland. There were no cruise ships or ferries in the northern part of the sea, only container ships. The shipping lane timetable was burnt into Minnow's memory like a tattoo beneath her skin. She'd made that trip every summer. Navigating for Minnow was like a dance between ship, wind, and sea. A dance she could do in her sleep. But commanding *The Seafarer* would not be easy. A sudden cloud of doubt whirled through her thoughts. *I'll be sailing over the deepest sea, in the darkest hour of the night.* She closed her eyes, trying not to think about the bottomless depths below her, or the creatures that might swim through it. Instead she thought of her grandma, Arielka, a woman who lived to go diving alone at night, in only a thin nightdress. Arielka was old in a way that felt knowledgeable with a heart made for dark storms. She had the lilting voice of a storyteller and a smile so jagged it could make you fear for your life. The image of the velvet box full of teeth flashed through Minnow's mind: *shark's teeth*. She shook the thought away, and pushed on into the night waters.

As the night wore on, Minnow found her confidence,

and the boat ploughed forward at a swift, fly-by-night speed. Minnow managed to push the image of Mercy disappearing to the edge of her memory and fill her mind only with the colour of starlight and the kiss of wind.

At last, the first rays of an Orcadian dawn gathered above their heads. Minnow was numb with exhaustion, but so glad to see light. She knew they'd travelled an extraordinary distance that other boats simply couldn't manage in the same timescale. But Minnow had learnt from the best, from a mother who paid no heed to rules, not even the nautical laws of wind speed. Mercy had taught Minnow from day one that belief alone could drive a ship across an ocean, regardless of time or tide. The following hours of the voyage were crucial and she couldn't afford to make a mistake. She needed to rest awhile. She gazed around for somewhere to dock, but could see nowhere. It was just too risky to lower the anchor here; if Miyuki wasn't strong enough to pull it back up they'd be stuck out at sea in plain sight. A boat such as *The Seafarer* was designed to steal the breath from all who saw it. Minnow didn't have time for hold-ups. She drew the sails in, her arms stiffening as though the salt had rusted her.

'Come on girl.' She smiled fondly. 'The boat can drift for the next half an hour. We need a break.' Instantly Miyuki broke her proud stance and bounded into the green silk hammock, eyes closing, tongue hanging out in a pant. Minnow could so easily have climbed in too and dozed on a pillow of Siberian fur. But though she was exhausted, Minnow felt too restless to sleep. She crept back inside the galley to the navigating table and gazed at the strange grey map. She had no idea what it was fashioned from, maybe camel or sharkskin or something worse like elephant. It definitely wasn't turtle hide or regular leather.

'How old are you?' Minnow murmured, tracing its landmarks with her fingers and finding it still cool. It seemed to hold the memory of oceans, the way a shell keeps whispers of the sea. Minnow stooped further over it. Then suddenly she knew exactly what it was made from: whale. Nothing else could glow underwater and remain clouded grey on land. It wasn't marked with any date or the cartographer's signature, but Minnow knew in her bones it was very old and special. *The Wild Deep*. She smiled, gazing at the faint lettering.

Minnow had been raised on stories and songs. Tales of underwater worlds where devilish sharks dwelt and sirens sang sailors to their deaths. Myths about unreachable oceans full of glittering secrets, creatures that were part child, part bird, or part fish. There were ballads for lost seas and lullabies for lost souls. But they were not nice heart-warming stories to read or sing before bed. They were fairy tales that could turn your blood cold. And always murmuring through all of them came the whisper of mermaids and a girl with shark's teeth.

The Sea Hunters or myth-chasers or whatever those men were, had claimed they had Mercy's teeth. But that was impossible, Minnow reasoned. The teeth in the velvet box were clearly not human, they belonged to some sort of small . . . shark. Minnow stood up and leaned over the sink, feeling quite sick. A memory was stirring from somewhere deep in her mind. The story of *The Girl with the Shark's Teeth*. It was one of the sea-myths her grandma had told her as a young child. Minnow couldn't quite remember it, but she knew that a girl with shark's teeth, who lives in an underwater kingdom, makes a terrible mistake by allowing herself to be seen by two drowning boys. She saves their lives and puts her own at risk. *But it's just a story.* Nausea pulsed through Minnow. She was feeling confused and exhausted, but too wired to sleep. She opened a high cupboard and took out a small pink bottle: her night medicine. This would at least help her to rest.

'I'll find Grandma,' she told herself, sinking into an armchair in the darkest part of the galley. 'She'll know what to do. We'll get mum away from the Sea Hunters and all of the strangeness will disappear.' And that was the last thought that stirred its way through Minnow's mind before sleep descended upon her and she was lost to the waking world.

A howl that could raise a tempest shattered Minnow's dream. Her eyes blinked open and she ran towards the sound. Miyuki stood on deck barking furiously as a thick grey fog slunk over the boat. Minnow shrank back slightly when she saw it. There was a ghostly quality to it that set her teeth on edge. 'Where are we?' she asked, scanning around for land. It was impossible to see anything through the dense dull air; at least if they had drifted ashore the mist would hide the boat's appearance. She crouched down beside the husky ruffling her fur, trying to calm both their nerves, but the barking wouldn't stop.

Snatched words and phrases from fairy tales swirled around Minnow's head. *A mist guards the waters of the Wild Deep, in which boats are lost forever.* She swallowed anxiously. *The Wild Deep's not real,* Minnow told herself, trying to think practically. How long had the mist been here? Minnow wasn't sure but the wind had ceased altogether. *What if we never get out of it?* She stumbled back inside the galley, hands over her ears trying to mute Miyuki's bark, and tried to power up her water-drenched phone, but it seemed her dip in the marina had finally killed it. She darted to the back of the galley and down the tight spiralling staircase which led to her cabin. It was half-moon shaped and painted in a delicate coral so when Minnow was in bed she felt like she was snuggled inside a huge conch shell. Minnow cursed when she saw that her alarm clock had also stopped. 'It must have run out of batteries,' she mumbled.

Minnow half fell into Mercy's cabin, a much larger half-moon painted in a deep indigo that echoed midnight rock pools. It was as much a study as a bedroom, consisting of a net-like hammock and a huge desk scattered with books, and papers, and strange and mysterious artefacts. Minnow brushed past the specimen of a dead Cambodian moth and looked to the ornate black clock that hung on the wall. It was crafted from wrought iron the same burnt tone as *The Seafarer*, and shaped like the star of the north. Each point of the star was dipped in metallic gold and bore another smaller clock which told another time from another place on the globe. It was incredibly useful for crossing time zones. *7.15 a.m.* the clock read. A deep frown crept across Minnow's face. She had slept for four hours. They could be anywhere . . . They might have drifted into rocks. They could have been swept out into a storm. And now they were lost in a ghostly mist.

Quite suddenly, and with alarming speed, two tiny doors just beneath the clock face burst open and a wooden swallow on a spring shot out, almost striking Minnow in the face. Her body moved before her mind could and she leapt in the air, giving a petrified scream as she overbalanced and tumbled to the floor. In seconds Miyuki was beside her, looping madly around her, licking her face in comfort. Minnow wound her arms around the dog's wild body. 'It's all right girl, it's just the clock,' she sighed, though her heart raced in her chest.

The painted swallow hung in the air above their heads and then the spring recoiled and the bird vanished back inside the clock. 'That's only supposed to happen on the hour. It must be broken,' thought Minnow, as she tramped back up towards the thickening mist, Miyuki in tow.

On deck the fog showed no sign of lifting. There was an uneasy silence that came with it and Minnow wanted out. 'What would Mama do, Miyuki?' she whispered, trying to shift the feeling of helplessness. She might put the anchor down and wait till the day cleared—but Minnow had no idea how deep the anchor might sink before it could still the boat. Or Mercy might sing. 'If the wind won't come to you then summon it with a song,' she would laugh, before climbing to the top of the mast, red hair flying like a flag, and singing to the sky. Whether by fate or chance it normally worked.

Minnow did not feel like singing—she felt more like crying or cursing. Her stupid teeth were hurting, as they often did when she was tired, and the feeling of being lost was making her deeply irritated, but she was beginning to feel desperate. Reluctantly, Minnow opened the sails, took a deep foggy breath, and started very quietly to chant a song, like a lullaby. Her lullaby. The one tune that could bring her comfort, even on nights when she dreamed of the beast, the same song she had heard Ely whistling on her ship the day before.

I am soul and song of water
I am fin and bone of star
I was dreamed from waves and moonlight
And my heart has swum so far.

The words were warm and familiar and soon Minnow started to enjoy them. She closed her eyes and threw her head back ready for the chorus,

for the call of the sea starts when you're young
And never stops chanting your name
Yes, the call of the sea starts when you're young
And never will you be the same.

Minnow felt the boat tug into motion beneath her feet. She keeled over in surprise, the song ceasing, the boat stilling. Miyuki hunkered down beside her, giving her a wet-nosed nudge. Minnow sat up and started singing again. Almost immediately the boat shifted, the sails billowing full, the air alive with sound. She clambered to her feet, trying to keep the song going and make sense of what was happening. It seemed as if the wind was full of wings. Minnow rushed to get Mercy's telescope and glanced madly at the sky. She was right; it wasn't just a wind, but a wind full of tiny feathered birds. Birds Minnow knew from the dip and soar of their arrow-like tails: swallows. Just like the little painted bird that had sprung from her mum's clock. Minnow didn't have time to question this miracle, she just had to keep singing.

Minnow sang for her life, and with a rush of feathers the birds were suddenly gone and a fierce wind was powering them on. A mountain range topped with white snow, dark as granite appeared on the horizon as the heavy fog cleared. It was unmistakably Mount Esja. Minnow held her breath, trying to process what she was seeing. Then she was yelling, dancing, skipping, a girl abounding with joy.

'Miyuki! Miyuki! It's Iceland, we've made it to Iceland!' Even as she shrieked Minnow couldn't fathom quite how this had happened, how they had drifted the exact route they needed to follow. How they had not met with anyone else. How they had travelled almost without wind. She collapsed into the hammock, her head spinning. *I must have slept all night . . . the boat must have kept travelling on course . . . the mist must have kept all other boats away from the water.* Minnow bit her lip, shuddering at how disastrous this could have been. She swore never to take a break again, ever, without casting the anchor or setting an alarm. Then she was up grabbing the wheel, steering firmly north, her smile full of the light of the sea. Soon they would be at Arielka's. She would make everything right.

As they neared the harbour, Miyuki gave a single swift howl of warning. Minnow lashed the wheel and darted to her side. She could see ahead a boy disappearing into the sea from a small fishing boat bobbing on the waves. She noticed his blue trainers as he vanished into the water. Minnow dived after him. She knew the dangers of swimming out deep; she knew that children can be lost to the sea, and she knew that she had to help him.

Chapter five

THE GREEN-EYED BOY

Salt water closed over Minnow's head and the sounds of the world disappeared. Even in fairest summer the Reykjavik sea was cold enough to make you gasp, but Minnow was practically immune to it. She searched through the pale greenness, curling down away from the light, hunting for the sinking boy. A flash of blue glimmered below and Minnow shot through the water at an astonishing speed, grabbing the boy's ankle with both hands then arcing upwards, her spine unfurling, her legs moving as one, so she broke the surface in a backwards dive, shooting into the air and dragging the boy with her.

He struck out in shock, kicking Minnow square in the face. 'Hey!' she spluttered, holding her cheek as the boy trod water in front of her, a terrible scowl on his face.

'What are you doing?' the boy demanded, flicking a

wave of blond hair out of his eyes, which were the same unsettled green as the sea.

Minnow swallowed, tasting blood, and instinctively ran her tongue over her loose tooth. It was one of her four silver ones: the boy must have knocked it when he kicked her. 'I'm saving your life,' she snapped. The boy snorted as if that was funniest thing he had ever heard.

'Well, what are you doing this far out?' Minnow asked carefully.

The boy rolled his eyes. 'Waiting to catch a legendary shark.' His English was flawless, his accent almost imperceptible except for the clipped manner with which he spoke.

'What about you?' he asked dryly. 'Searching for the Northern Lights? Hunting for elves?'

Minnow frowned uncomfortably. 'No, I'm visiting my grandmother,' she answered, glancing over at the boy's boat and noticing that it was full of diving equipment. At once Minnow realized her mistake. The boy was skilled at sea. He definitely did not need rescuing. Blushing painfully she mumbled an explanation. 'Look, I just thought . . . because of your shoes . . . you might need help . . . '

The boy gave a blink of confusion. 'My shoes? These are classic hi-tops—they're the coolest thing I own.'

Minnow cut him off. 'Well, don't wear them in the sea. I thought you were in trouble.'

The boy smirked and turned back towards his boat, calling to her over his shoulder. 'I'm practising for the national ice-diving championships. My shoes have got weights in . . . But you wouldn't get it. It's not really a tourist thing . . .'

'Weighted shoes?' Minnow had never heard of anything so ridiculous in all her life. 'Well, try not to drown,' she shouted after him, sarcastically, before diving below the water.

Beneath the sea she felt calmer. The rhythm was rough and accepting and the song of the sea was soft but clear. *Who was that awful green-eyed boy?* Minnow was half tempted to shoot really deep and not resurface for a good ten minutes. That would shut him up. Of course she knew what the national ice-diving championships were. One Christmas, when she'd been a lot younger, Arielka had playfully entered Minnow, and she'd shocked everyone by winning. Beating many serious sea-swimming adults who'd trained all year. None of the Reykjavik locals could believe it: their trophy was taken by a child of five, a little brown girl with untameable hair who could barely stand up on her own. They had regarded her with nervous astonishment. Mercy had been furious and banned Minnow from ever taking part again, but Arielka had been wickedly triumphant.

Minnow grinned underwater and sought out the dark shape of her home. The hull loomed above her like a shadow. Almost without thinking, Minnow calculated the distance between her and the stern of the boat. She dived deeper into the sea, then began to race up towards the surface, swimming mainly with the motion of her back and dolphin-like kick of her legs, gaining speed with every heartbeat. She emerged, a whirlwind of sea and girl, landing in a crouch on the deck of her home. Miyuki bounded to greet her and Minnow wound her wet braids into a knot, took up the wheel and began steering the boat towards Reykjavik's tiny Old Harbour.

The green-eyed boy stared in amazement as Minnow shot out of the water and landed perfectly on board. She was fast as an orca hunting a bird. Then the boy's gaze fell upon the boat and he almost stopped breathing. Here was a vessel of black sails and dark wood stolen straight from a pirate's dream. He could do nothing but open and close his mouth like a fish pulled from the surf. Long after Minnow had guided *The Seafarer* into the tiny harbour, the boy remained transfixed, unable to take his eyes from the silhouette on the horizon. And he began to wonder about the girl who had dragged him to the surface. Who was she? Did she live on that boat all alone? He would go home and speak to his mum. She was an artist, and curator at the National Museum. Her exhibitions were mostly of sunken boats that she rescued from the Scandinavian coast or raised up from the graveyard of ships. Maybe she'd know where the black ship originated from? And if she didn't know, surely Old Gunnar or Mad Elka would.

As Minnow docked in Reykjavik's quaint harbour, the day was full of sea air and the overpowering smell of fresh fish. Minnow found herself beaming at the colourful storybook houses before her. This little city with a fierce northern heart was her second home. But it was the first time she had ever been here without her mama. Minnow shot into motion. She seized the painter, a huge length of rope, and wound it round her waist, whistling shrilly to Miyuki as she did so. Then she leapt onto the walkway, scuffing her wet toes and swearing. Together Minnow and Miyuki bound the huge boat to the dock, with a double figure-of-eight knot. Then they set off at a jog through the neat little streets.

The city was alive with summer. Cafés bustled with the clink of coffee cups, gangs of children roamed freely, and families lingered around the world-famous hot dog stand. All of them noticed Minnow and some of them paused to stare. But Minnow was quite used to this gentle fascination. Even though Brighton was a melting pot of cultures, she'd been the only mixed-race girl both at ballet and trampolining. There were Black, Asian, European, and Russian children, but none who looked precisely like her. At her old school there were some twins who'd been adopted who had Minnow's exact same skin tone, and a family of three lively brothers who were mixed Irish-Jamaican. The youngest boy had the same hair. But nobody had Minnow's silver teeth, nor the barely visible scars on her neck. And nobody seemed to struggle with the world in quite the same way she did. *Weird bones are hardly the start of it,* thought Minnow darkly. For a lot of the time she felt . . . *What?* Restless. Like a sail teased by the wind. Or as if she were circling the edge of her city, not quite in it. She was only ever really at home in the sea.

Finally she saw Arielka's yellow house. It was a faint sunshine colour, with symmetrical white shutters that made it look as though it belonged to a family of dolls. You wouldn't have guessed that inside were six different flats. Minnow's grandmother's was on the second floor, with a rusted ladder leading from the back bedroom directly down and into the North Atlantic. Minnow and her dog flew up the stairs, hammering desperately on the door. There was no answer. Minnow fished around in the pocket of her shorts pulling out the whaleskin map, her sealskin purse, her now dead phone, her mum's locket, and finally a set of jangling keys. Quickly she unlocked the door and called her grandmother's name, but the little flat was still and quiet as a lake. The tiny red-finned sharks that circled inside their tank, no bigger than the width of your hand, eyed the girl and the dog silently.

Minnow hurried to the window, scanning the horizon for a lone figure swimming far out, but there was only the gleaming white surf. Miyuki barked impatiently and Minnow flopped down on her grandmother's hanging couch. Miyuki needed feeding, Minnow needed breakfast and maybe a warm bath, and the two of them needed a moment to catch their breath. *Then we'll find Grandma.* Minnow knew all her grandmother's favourite spots, and Miyuki could search through the lava fields if they needed to. She took a deep swig of air, the kind of breath you would take before diving to the depths of a bottomless ocean, then raised herself up and went to find her and Miyuki something to eat.

Six hours later Minnow's patience was thinning to dust. Her grandmother was not at the ice cream parlour or Laugardalslaug open-air swimming pool, nor was she at Kaldi Bar, the gin palace, or any of the coffee shops she loved. Minnow felt uneasy, like a sailor who has been at sea too long and forgotten how to navigate land. She crouched down on the dark rocks beside the Harpa concert hall and buried her face in Miyuki's deep, silvery fur, the drum of that steady heart her only stability. 'Where is she hiding?' she hissed through her teeth. But there was no more searching to do; she would have to go back to the yellow house and wait. Minnow wasn't good at waiting. It implied that you had to stay still and that was simply impossible. She was better off moving, circling the city and keeping the flat in sight at all times.

'Come on, Miyuki,' Minnow groaned, heading towards the harbour trying to keep hopeful, one hand gently twisting the husky's winter fur.

They lingered at the bookshop, bought a smoothie from the Laundromat Café, and popped into an overpriced convenience store to get batteries for Minnow's alarm clock. All the while her heart thrummed with unease, but she swallowed it down and tried to think practically. They were just leaving the shop when Miyuki gave a sudden moonstruck howl. Minnow looked up to see a light on in Arielka's flat.

The front door of the flat flew open before Minnow could reach it, and there stood her grandmother. Minnow skidded to a stop. Arielka looked so pale and so tired, it left Minnow speechless.

Even on the mildest summer day, Arielka could draw frowns from people. Her skin was pallid as a winter moon, so thin in places it had become translucent, much like that of a very young fish. Beneath the leather gloves she always wore were patches of skin so clear you could see right through to the blood in her veins. And then there were her teeth. They were green from years of smoking seaweed, and had grown at disconcerting angles, so that when Arielka smiled directly at you, it gave the sense of something deeply unhuman looking you in the eye and wanting to kill you. Yes, there was something murderous about her mouth. But she was normally a life force of merriment and gin. A formidable figure who climbed down her ladder in the middle of the night and swam out to save storm-struck fishermen from drowning. Yet the woman before Minnow looked as though she was ready to lie down at the bottom of the sea and sleep forever.

'Grandma,' Minnow gulped, trying to shake her shock away and collapsing into Arielka's arms. The sharp scent of salt and lemons mixed with Chanel perfume surrounded Minnow. It was a smell like home and childhood, and at once she felt safe.

'What a wonderful surprise,' Arielka cooed.

'Where've you been?' Minnow gasped.

'At the doctor's, out of town,' said Arielka with a dismissive flick of her long grey hair. She ran her softly-gloved fingers through Minnow's braids and Minnow could have stayed forever in the warmth of her grandmother's embrace.

'It's Mum,' she began quietly.

'What about her?' Arielka beamed, peering over Minnow's shoulder. 'Where is she?'

'She's been taken away,' Minnow began.

'Mercy isn't with you?' Arielka asked, drawing herself up to her most elegant height, her shadow stretching away from her, as if it longed to escape to the sea. 'Then who is my daughter with?' she said slowly, her liquid grey eyes fixed on Minnow.

Minnow began twisting her hair. It was such an odd question: not *where* is Mercy but *who* is Mercy with?

'Three men,' Minnow mumbled, feeling her blood go cold. 'They came to our boat, and said she could help them find a mermaid, then they put her in a car to the airport . . . '

Arielka moved to the window giving a long rushing sigh.

'I know their names. Jah Jah, Ely, and Louis. Who are they? What's this about?' Minnow stammered, feeling her throat begin to close. Arielka turned to her with such a grave look, Minnow had to grip the windowsill to stop herself from running.

'There are many things we should have told you . . . ' she began, taking Minnow's face in her hands and looking at her strangely. 'Do you believe in magic?'

'What are you talking about, Grandma?' Minnow asked, pulling the whaleskin map from her pocket and thrusting it at Arielka. 'Mum gave me this. What does it mean?'

The old woman regarded the map fondly, a look of quiet wonder crossing her face. Then another voice spoke up from the corner.

'Wow. What a cool map.'

Minnow almost fainted with shock. For standing in the doorway to the kitchen was the awful green-eyed boy.

Chapter Six

THE BOOK OF FAIRY TALES

Arielka turned to the boy. 'Raife. This is my beloved granddaughter, Minnow.'

Raife stared at Minnow as a slow realization dawned on his face.

Minnow stared back at Raife. He was literally the last person in all of Iceland, possibly the world, that she wanted to see. 'Why is he here?' she breathed.

'Raife delivers my goods from the flea market, bits of dried fish, bottles of black death,' said Arielka calmly, 'and in return I share my knowledge of sharks with him.'

Minnow cut her off: 'Make him leave.'

Arielka sagely shook her head. 'Be still your storm, little fish. You can trust Raife—he might be able to help.'

Minnow did not see how this could possibly be the case, but she was wise enough not to argue with her grandmother. She stalked into the kitchen and sank onto a stool, Miyuki softly resting her chin on Minnow's lap. Raife tried not to look at the sullen girl or her beautiful dog, and stared around the softly-lit kitchen instead.

'Minnow's mother has disappeared,' Arielka began, sweeping across the room with such swiftness that Raife had the sudden notion he was going to be attacked.

'Why are you telling a stranger about Mama?' Minnow seethed, banging both her fists on the table. Arielka shot her a look that brought silence.

Raife cleared his throat and drew his stool closer to the table. Reading between the lines, he already sensed that calling the police was not the way, here. 'Gunnar would lend me his boat and my stepdad Viktor's pretty fast on his bicycle: we could get a search party going?'

Minnow shook her head with such mad fury one of her plaits struck Raife in the eye. 'Mum's not in Reykavik!' she hissed. And in that moment, she was so like Mercy that Arielka couldn't help but give a little crooked smile.

'Well, when did you last see your mother?' Raife began, straightening on his stool.

'She left the boat. She went off with some men. And I just can't understand why,' Minnow growled.

'She was protecting you, Minnow,' said Arielka slowly. 'Those men don't know you exist. And if they find out, they might come for you instead.'

Minnow bit her lip. One of the men, *Ely*, clearly did

know about her but he had pretended not to. He had tried to warn Mercy even though she didn't listen. Beside her, Raife almost toppled off his stool in astonishment. He had never imagined that a trip to Mad Elka's would involve a plot about an actual kidnap. 'And you don't know who the men are, or what they want?'

'No,' Minnow sighed, and as the light fell across her face Raife glimpsed her four silver-bright teeth. 'I think maybe the men are Sea Hunters and they think my mum can lead them to a . . . ' Minnow faltered for a second—it seemed crazy to say it out loud to a stranger—and one she didn't trust at that. Raife gave her an encouraging grin and she took a breath. 'They think my mum can lead them to a mermaid.'

Raife was stunned into silence.

Arielka left the room in a swish of satin, returning moments later with an old dusty book. Minnow sat up straighter. It was a book she knew and loved, its faded turquoise cover worn with age and speckled with tea stains and rum. *The Book of Sea-Myths: Tales of the Sea.* It was a book which held every story, song, and fairy tale that made up Minnow's childhood. Though she knew many of the stories by heart, she had never read them for herself, because the entire book was written in Old Norse.

Arielka opened the book and handed it to Raife. 'You may begin.'

Minnow gazed at him in surprise. 'You can read Old Norse?'

Raife gave a shy nod. He wasn't exactly keen on reading, nor translating. But he didn't feel bold enough to disobey Mad Elka. Nervously Raife began to read.

'*Long ago in the waters of the Wild Deep, a girl with shark's teeth and a young Merfin set off on a forbidden adventure. Hand in hand they dived to uncharted depths and approached the Gate between Somertide in the Wild Deep and the ocean beyond.*

'*The Gate from the Wild Deep had a Keeper, as enchanted waterways often do: a fearsome protector to guard it. But the girl and the Merfin were both keen-eyed and mischievous, with hearts as quick as the break of a wave and bright as a soaring gull. They waited till the Gatekeeper was distracted, and in that rare moment they sang the Gate open and slipped gloriously through.*

'*Up to the Far Above they raced, carried on a tide of courage and joy. When the sun-dazzled surface broke around them, they found themselves in the waters of the Caribbean Sea. The sky was blue with summer wonders, the tide still as a lake. There wasn't a boat in sight. They raced and twirled and dipped with delight, keeping their*

distance from the island of Barbados, a haze of gold on their horizon.

'Now, on the shores of Barbados at that very moment, two young brothers were haggling for a boat. They had given up their shoes, they had given away a stolen wheelbarrow, they had even parted with a watch they had won in a game of cards. Eventually the fishermen agreed that the boys could borrow one of the small fishing boats and keep it only if they could bring back a reef shark. The small wooden fishing boat was barely seaworthy. Its single sail was ripped and its old oars worn slim from the grip of many hands. But the bottom of the boat was crafted from glass, like a window to the soul of the sea. The brothers believed this boat could change their fortune. All they had to do was catch a reef shark and the boat would be theirs. Neither boy was a strong swimmer, but this did not concern them. They had a sea as flat as a mirror and courage in their blood. And like all spirited children, they thought themselves immortal.

'But tides can turn. As the boys rowed across the tranquil waters, the shark-tooth girl and the Merfin began to play a game of dares. The Merfin beat the sea with her tail, making waves break in stunning

iridescence. The shark-tooth girl stirred the surf with her voice, making the water whirl into violent pools. Then the Merfin dived deep, drawing the water into a swooping current. The girl with the shark's teeth laughed mercilessly, raised her arms to the skies and sang to the High Winds. At once the day became the colour of thunder and the rain came down like knives. The world turned black and lightning crackled. The shark-tooth girl and the Merfin roared with glee, for storms were their wildest pleasure.

'They did not see the small wooden boat approach. They did not see the huge hand-stitched net. They did not see the two boys clinging to one another in fear, nor the look of bewilderment that struck their young faces when they spotted a creature with a glittering tail.

'Suddenly the Merfin was caught in the net, her beautiful tail bound tight with thread. She screamed in fury and arced below, struggling to break free. A wave crashed against the boat, pulling the boys overboard, and the net tangled dangerously around them as they were dragged beneath the surface.

'The sea became darker, and death was almost upon them. The Merfin soared towards the Gate, her heart a

ball of terror. She sang, but her voice was so ragged with fright that the Gate between worlds didn't open. Then her friend, the girl with the shark's teeth, cut through the sea like a bolt of moonlight. She sliced the net with her pointed teeth and sang with a voice of waves and wishes, opening the magical waterway. The Merfin flitted through, never to cross to the Far Above again. The fearless shark-tooth girl caught the two drowning boys in her arms. This was her storm, her mistake to undo. She could not let them die. So she broke every rule of Old Sea Magic and she saved their tender lives.

'When the boys' boat washed up on the beach, with them inside, they were heralded heroes for surviving the storm. Their family and friends had never looked so thankful to see them, and by way of a gift they were given the boat without the exchange of a shark.

'When they claimed that a mermaid nearly drowned them and a girl with teeth like a shark had saved them, the islanders fell about laughing. All except for their little sister who found a sharp and luminous scale snared within the net, along with a handful of scarlet hair. The older boy wore the scale round his neck, a reminder of the many wonders of the deep. The younger boy bound the

strands of red hair into a bracelet, adorned with cowrie shells, like medals of honour, an ode to the sea.

'They did not forget the girl nor the Gate. They grew up in the shadow of this memory, their dreams ever coloured by the secrets of the ocean beyond the Gate. At night their hearts held out for a song. A ballad of salt and sunken moons sung by a girl with shark's teeth.

'Many years passed and the boys grew into young men. The younger brother remained a quiet, peaceful soul, who spent his time catching fish and navigating by starlight, still captivated by the memories of his childhood. The older brother became a brutal Sea Hunter, who fought and stole and plundered the waves, searching for the gateway to the Wild Deep, determined to capture a mermaid.

'One night a blue moon rose over Barbados and the tide crept back revealing the Gate. The young men sailed forth, their hearts so light they almost soared. They sang and whistled and chanted the song they had heard the girl sing but alas the Gate would not open. They needed the girl with the shark's teeth to sing it for them.

'Night after night the brothers pursued this dream, until finally, when the moon turned blue once more,

they found her. But the girl had grown into a woman far fiercer than a human mind can imagine. A daughter of daggers and bone. A defender of the Wild Deep as merciless as the sea. She threw the two brothers overboard into the same deadly waters she had once saved them from. And then, to protect the gateway to the Deep, she wrenched the teeth from her mouth, dismantling her magic and swimming away.

'All that washed up on the beach the next morning were six small shark's teeth.

'Nobody knows what became of the brothers, or the mysterious girl. Some say the brothers roamed the bottom of the sea as lonesome ghosts. Some say they pursued the girl across oceans, singing her own song to haunt her. Some say the girl turned the brothers into mermen. One thing is for certain: the brothers never did go through the Gate and the mysteries of the Wild Deep were kept safe.

'And that is why you must honour the sea, for it is stranger and wilder than we ever shall know and it will never give up its secrets.'

A quietness had descended upon the kitchen. The three people in it regarded one another. For Raife, the tale rang with truth. Not that he believed in strange creatures who sang underwater to open magical gates. But he understood the secretive nature of oceans. How the things you see out late at night in a small fishing boat can seem like magic. How easily you could become enchanted by something that lived beneath the surface.

For Minnow the tale brought a swift sense of bewilderment. Her grandmother had told her this story as a child, of course. But it wasn't *real*. Yet all she could think of was the glowing pendant around Jah Jah's neck. The velvet box full of teeth. The bracelet on Ely's wrist, held together with scarlet thread. Or maybe hair.

Minnow turned to Arielka. 'Is it real, Grandma?'

Arielka smiled a sad and distant smile. 'Yes, my darling. The Wild Deep is a real ocean. A sea within a sea. You dive deep to enter its Gate at Vintertide, then swim to a place of waves and sky, icebergs and islands. It is home to many marvels, Minnow, stranger than you dare imagine.'

Both Minnow and Raife were still, the silence stretching out between them as they did both dare to imagine. 'And mermaids . . . ?' asked Minnow after a time.

Arielka gave a slow deliberate nod. 'Yes, my darling, they are real.'

Chapter Seven

THE GATEKEEPER'S DAUGHTER

'There have always been Mer.' Arielka's voice was low and dangerous, but soft as a wave. 'They have swum through the seas of every time and culture, and have as many names as the night: Merrow, Ondine, Selkie, Siren. But those who dwell in the Wild Deep have always been known as Merfins.'

Minnow found herself smiling at this. *Merfin*. It was a name that rang with enchantment. 'So those men . . . believe mum can help them catch a Merfin?'

'The fairy tale doesn't tell the whole story, Minnow. And I think you already know that the girl with the shark's teeth is your mama, and the brothers didn't perish in the sea but survived. Ely and Jah Jah have been pursuing your mother for most of her life. They want much more than simply to catch a Merfin,' said Arielka, as if that in itself might be easy. 'They want to enter the Wild Deep.'

Raife blinked in amazement. 'Why?' he breathed, even though really it was obvious why. If he'd been a boy in a borrowed boat, had accidentally caught a mermaid, half drowned, got rescued by a shark-toothed girl and glimpsed the Gate to the Wild Deep, he would want to go back. I mean, of course he would.

Arielka sighed. 'When the brothers discovered the Wild Deep, it affected them in different ways. Ely, the quieter boy, was touched with wonder. It was enough for him to know that such a place existed. He only wanted to befriend your mother and help protect the secret. Jah Jah, the louder, fearless little soul was drawn so strongly to the dream of finding a mermaid—again—it took over his whole life. He became an excellent diver and a world-renowned treasure hunter.

'For a while when they were young, Jah Jah, Ely, and your mama became friends. Mercy met the boys in the Far Above even though she knew it was forbidden and they learned to dive deeper, swim stronger. But their desire to cross the Gate never faded and eventually Mercy realized that she had to protect the Wild Deep and could no longer be friends with the brothers. Ely understood. Jah Jah did not.'

'So what do they want with Mama now?' asked Minnow, a terrible sense of foreboding gathering in her spine.

'In three days the blue moon will rise over Barbados revealing the Gate once more, and Jah Jah will force your mother to sing.'

Minnow frowned, trying to straighten everything out in her head. 'So the Sea Hunters think Mama can open the Gate with a song?'

Arielka nodded. 'She can.' There was a pause as the two children tried to absorb this.

'What about the teeth?' asked Raife after a moment.

'Yes,' cried Minnow, thinking again of the velvet box. If those shark's teeth really *were* Mercy's then maybe when she pulled them out she *did* dismantle the magic. 'Can Mama still open the Gate without her teeth?'

The old woman's eyes twinkled so sadly that Minnow felt her heart lurch. 'The Gate will open regardless. When Mercy pulled her teeth out it was just for show, a way to throw Jah Jah off. A way to belong in the Far Above once and for all.'

'So Mama sings, the Gate opens, and the Sea Hunters are free to just catch a mermaid,' Minnow mused, impatiently chewing her plait. 'She'll never do it.'

'No,' Arielka agreed, 'she will not. She will defend the Deep and refuse to sing, and Jah Jah will probably try to kill her.'

Raife fell off his stool, mumbling an apology that nobody seemed to hear.

'Of course, Mercy is too skilled. Jah Jah will never

succeed,' Arielka added with a wry smile.

But Minnow wasn't listening. 'How can we stop him? How can we get to Barbados before the blue moon?'

Raife grabbed his phone and quickly began checking. 'There are no direct flights . . . You have to go to New York then change.'

'How much will that cost?' Minnow was almost screaming.

Raife's expression was grave: at this short notice it was more money than he imagined he'd ever own.

'We'll never get there,' Minnow wailed.

'Unless you sail,' said Raife. 'I mean you've got a pretty awesome boat.'

Minnow looked at him, catching his earnest green eyes with a thankful glance. 'Yes! How long will that take? I mean it's . . . We'd have to get to the Caribbean Sea . . . And then . . . ' Gradually Minnow whirred to a stop. 'We'll never get there in three days,' she uttered completely defeated.

'You might get there,' said Raife carefully. He was studying the whaleskin map. 'If you were willing to cross the Wild Deep.'

Arielka opened her old grey eyes very wide, and abruptly cleared her throat, but neither of the children noticed. Minnow frowned at Raife in confusion.

'This is a coastline,' he explained, pointing to the Vintertide edge of the map. A small white structure was marked and beneath it an entrance of some sort had been sketched, like an inward waterfall. 'And that's the lighthouse Lumière.' Raife pointed to the white structure. 'Lots of folk think it's a myth but I've seen it when I've been early morning fishing with Old Gunnar. I think it would lead you to the Vintertide Gate.'

A fragment of the story danced through Minnow's mind.

One unexpected night a blue moon rose over Barbados and the tide crept back revealing the Gate.

'There must be two Gates to the Wild Deep!' she exclaimed, studying the map. 'We could go through the Gate at Vintertide, cross Darkentide and then out through the Gate at Somertide, bringing us out in the Caribbean Sea!'

'Yes,' Raife agreed, his green eyes becoming very bright. 'This island,' he said, spinning the map around and pointing to a spattering of golden sand beyond the Somertide border, 'is the west coast of Barbados.'

Minnow shot to her feet. 'Are you sure?'

Raife nodded eagerly. 'I'm sure that's Death Rock Cove,' he answered. 'It's a marker for treasure hunters; some of the best shipwrecks in the world have sunk below it. It's near Speightstown. I saw a documentary on it.'

Minnow felt her heart beat faster. 'So if we could

open the Vintertide Gate, then maybe we really could reach Barbados before the blue moon?'

She thought of everything she knew about the waters of the Wild Deep. It was an enchanted ocean, supposedly home to all sorts of sea creatures, some mythical, some long forgotten, some yet to be discovered. Children with feathered wingspans and beaks. Little beasts who looked human until they opened their mouths. Creatures with fingers of clawed coral and folk with green skin. It was a sea of many marvels. Yet Minnow knew it was also an ocean dark with danger.

'Grandma? Could we cross the Wild Deep in three days?'

Arielka smoothed the frown from her pale brow, took a small sheet of seaweed, packed it with tobacco and started rolling it neatly into a cigarette.

'Maybe,' she said slowly, 'if you knew how to dive deeper than you ever have before, and if you knew how to open the Vintertide and Somertide Gates, and if you knew how to charm the winds.'

Minnow couldn't breathe. 'You could teach me Grandma; we could do it together.'

The old woman raised a gloved hand. 'I cannot allow it.'

Minnow gave a huge, exasperated sigh. 'Why not?'

Arielka pushed her seaweed cigarette into an elaborate holder, lit it, and inhaled the sweet green smoke. 'Do you remember that there is a Gatekeeper, who keeps watch over the entrances to the Wild Deep?' Her voice was smooth as silk.

'Yes,' Minnow and Raife answered at once.

'Well, Mercy grew up to become a Gatekeeper between worlds. Before she gave it all up, it was her greatest joy.'

'Is that why she couldn't stay friends with the brothers?' asked Raife.

'The Sea Hunters,' scowled Minnow.

Arielka gave a sharp nod. 'Becoming a Gatekeeper is a game of skill and impossible luck. You need three things:

'1) You must be able to pass.'

Minnow screwed up her eyes trying to recall what 'passing' meant. Then it came to her, a sentence borne on breath of waves: *In the Wild Deep a creature more human than fish could sometimes pass between oceans.* Someone who looked human.

'2) You must be able to fight to the death: only the shark bloodline has the heart for it.'

The shark bloodline? What did that mean? That not only did her mum have shark teeth, but shark blood? Shark bones? A terrible feeling began to creep over Minnow. *Weird Bones . . . Malleable . . . Unbreakable. Just like a shark . . . And so what did that make her? Minnow gulped and turned back to her grandmother.*

'3) The Gate must choose you.'

The Gate summons a new Keeper every generation, and for that time she or he is bound to the Gate beyond all other ties. You must sacrifice everything—family, friendship, love—nothing comes before the Gate.'

Arielka lowered her eyes and peeled off her leather gloves. Raife tried not to wince at the clear patches of skin on her wrists, through which he was sure he could see the gleam of her bones. 'You must never have children. At least not while the Gate is in your care.'

Minnow felt the room begin to close in around her. She was on land, she knew, but she felt as if a dark tide was rising, engulfing her.

'You mean I'm the reason Mama can never go back there?' Minnow was struggling to draw breath. A sharp, twisted thought gnawed at her heart and she stumbled back knocking a vase over, hardly noticing as it smashed over her feet. 'Why have I got these silver teeth, Grandma?'

Arielka rose and pulled Minnow into her arms, surrounding her with the scent of lemons and seaweed smoke. 'You are like your mother in so many ways,' she said gently. But Minnow could only stare and blink, all words lost to her.

Raife shifted awkwardly on his stool, but his eyes were dancing with excitement. 'What happened when Mercy abandoned the Gate?'

'I don't know,' said Arielka stiffly. 'When Mercy left the Wild Deep I had to leave too, or risk never seeing my daughter again.'

Minnow pushed her hair out of her face and heaved a sigh. 'So what are we supposed to do—just wait here and hope Mama is OK?'

'Exactly that,' Arielka said, soothingly.

'But there must be something we can do to stop those wretched men.'

Arielka chuckled darkly. 'Don't be too hard on them, little fish. They are not the first to fall in love with the Wild Deep and all its secrets, nor will they be the last.'

'So what am I supposed to do while we wait?'

'We'll keep busy,' Arielka instructed.

'Raife can take you to the flea market, translate more of the book.'

Minnow banged the table again, absolutely fuming. 'I don't want to go the flea market! I want to sail across the Wild Deep and rescue Mama.'

Arielka turned and spoke only to Raife: 'Perhaps it's time you headed home.'

Her voice wasn't unkind but it certainly wasn't a question. Raife reluctantly stood up, gave a quick nod of goodbye and headed for the stairs.

As he stepped out into the light summer twilight, still un-dark at ten o'clock, a voice called after him soft as a shell, 'Goodbye Raife . . . thanks.'

He turned to see Minnow standing at the top of the stairs, her brown eyes sparkling sadly. He held up a hand and she waved back, flashing him a fleeting smile. The way her entire face became full of sea-light was so joyful that Raife found he had to smile back. Then suddenly he was urgently beckoning to her, taking Minnow by the hand, and guiding her away from the house into the quiet of the street. 'You could do it you know. You could cross the Wild Deep, if the wind was in your favour.'

Minnow blinked at Raife in surprise. 'But I don't know how deep I would have to dive, or how to get through the Gate, or charm the winds.'

'You're the Gatekeeper's daughter. Can you get me the book? I bet the song you need to sing is in there.'

Minnow's bones at once felt lighter. She was dizzy, not from lack of air, but from the faint summoning of an adventure. 'If we knew the song, would you help me find the Gate?' The words felt like ice on Minnow's tongue. Could she really just sing a song and sail to a mystical ocean?

'Sure,' said Raife casually.

'Meet me at the harbour at midnight,' Minnow replied. And just like that the future became set, like a course you chart to the stars. There was a quest, a direction, a way to get to the Wild Deep. *A way to get to Mama.*

Chapter Eight

THE LIGHTHOUSE LUMIÈRE

By a quarter to midnight *The Seafarer* was loaded and ready to set sail. Minnow had crept back into the little flat, trying not to glitter with the knowledge of secrets. She'd moved around the kitchen, tidying up the broken vase, sweeping away seaweed ash, and lighting candles. Arielka had called out just once to her before she drifted to sleep on the hanging couch. 'In the deepest dark, Minnow, you must be the light.' It was the one thing her grandmother always said to her whenever the dream of the dark sea beast struck.

'OK, Grandma.' Minnow felt a pang of guilt as she tucked the ancient book beneath her t-shirt and tiptoed out of the flat as her grandmother slept.

Now here she was in the darkened harbour, battening

down *The Seafarer* so that if a storm were to hit, *or we sailed into a magical ocean,* nothing would shatter. It meant that everything had to be locked away. She had studied the whaleskin map once more and found her grandma was right: the Wild Deep was almost a mirror image of the Far Above. Sky as well as sea and clumps of land all existed down there, in a secret world all of its own. But she would have to dive down deep first. Deeper than ever before. And then open the Gate. Minnow looked around. It was one thing for a girl to dive down into the Deep, but what about her ship, and what about Raife and her beloved Miyuki? Minnow hoped the answers would become clearer on the journey ahead.

Minnow ran through everything she knew about the Gate:

It was deep beneath the waves.

Only a special song would open it.

It had a Keeper.

Minnow wasn't afraid of diving deep, and holding her breath came easily, but she was afraid of diving into the darkest depths of the ocean. Of entering the inky gloom which swirls through seemingly bottomless oceans without a glimmer of light. She tossed her head from side to side, trying to shake the thought away.

At least we should be able to figure out the song—Raife would help. Minnow closed her eyes and tried to imagine singing underwater and for some reason this part didn't feel daunting. Her dreams, when they weren't haunted by the beast at the bottom of the ocean, were often full of music. Whale song, dolphin chatter, the rushing of bright waves. Sometimes Minnow dreamed herself into these water-bound melodies, as if she were singing them at the bottom of a clear, bright sea. Her song had made her ship move once before, so why shouldn't she open the Gate?

The thought of the Gatekeeper, though, was bothering her most of all. *What if they don't let me pass?* A sentence from the book sparkled in her mind.

They waited till the Gatekeeper was distracted, and in that rare moment they sang the Gate open and slipped gloriously through.

Minnow pictured her mother young and fearless, hand in hand with a mermaid, outwitting the Gatekeeper. 'Mama got out of the Gate,' she said determinedly, 'so surely I can get in?' Miyuki quietly watched her from the corner, her wolf ears cocked to the wind. 'Besides,' Minnow reassured herself, 'there are two gates. The Keeper can't be at both of them—maybe the Gatekeeper won't even be there?'

The echo of footsteps crossing the half lit harbour

interrupted Minnow's thoughts. *Raife is really here. This is really happening. We are actually going to sail to the Wild Deep.* She bound her plaits into a knot and hurried to the deck. Her home looked so surreal with only the whaleskin map and the starfish paperweight on the navigation table and with everything else packed away. She laid a hand on the empty wall, wondering what stories its dark wood could tell.

Outside, Raife found he was silently ecstatic. This was it. This was the dream and he was living it. He was boarding a pirate ship to search out a legendary lighthouse. All of the pre-dawn trips out at sea in ancient, leaky fishing boats; the rushing bumpiness of small motorboats that had rescued him and Old Gunnar from sudden, unstoppable storms; the occasional two-person sailing boat they'd dared to try and reach Greenland in; the many trips to the graveyard of boats with his mother, and the amazing, unforgettable moments where he had been lucky enough to glimpse the legendary Greenland shark lighting up the dark waters below him: Raife couldn't help but feel that all of that had been in preparation for this moment. A seemingly unknown mission on a ship of imposing majesty with a girl he'd kicked in the face only that morning. Never had he imagined his day would go this way.

He glanced up at Minnow. She was positioned protectively at the front of the ship near the wooden mermaid, looking just as fierce. Her Salt-water sandals were gone and instead she wore silver sequin Converse, and a small sou'wester in sunshine yellow. Raife hesitated a moment wondering if he should say hi, or hey, or Yo ho ho but there seemed no words big enough to capture how he felt. So instead he just saluted, which was a little awkward, but it made Minnow smile and she waved *Tales of the Sea* triumphantly in the air and beckoned him into the galley.

Two flickering lanterns cast an orange glow around the room and Raife perched at the table pouring over the fairy tale book. Minnow sat opposite him gazing again at the whaleskin map. *The Wild Deep* . . .

After some time Raife looked up, slightly paler than before. 'I can't find anything about the song . . . ' he muttered, a little downcast.

Minnow thought back to the marina and to Ely. He had been whistling a song: *my sea lullaby*. She pictured herself singing that very song on the boat that morning, the wind stirring around her, parting the mist, and she felt a sharp rush of joy.

'I think I've got it.'

'Really?' said Raife, looking doubtful. He was sure a Gate such as the one to the Wild Deep wouldn't just open for any old karaoke number.

Minnow took a deep breath, closed her eyes, and began.

I am soul and song of water
I am fin and bone of star
I was dreamed from waves and moonlight
And my heart has swum so far.

A slow wind whistled through Reykjavik. A wind of secrets and promises lost to the sea. It tumbled through the streets, dancing with church bells and snowflake wind chimes, kissing the cheeks of sleeping children, until it reached the harbour where it rattled the rigging. And then it found the huge black sails of Minnow's home, shrieking into being, driving the boat into the open water. Miyuki gave a windswept howl and both children nearly fell over in amazement.

'You actually summoned the wind with a song, like magic,' murmured Raife, spellbound. 'That must be the song that opens the Gate. I mean it has to be.'

Minnow nodded, her heart so full with glee she felt she could have floated. A small wave hit the boat and she sprang into sailing mode, trimming the sails in, freeing ropes, ducking under beams and flying up and down rope ladders with an accuracy that was astounding. Raife took up the role of lookout, secretly watching Minnow in the flare of his pocket torch, studying her shadow to see if in fact she had wings. But she did not. She was simply a girl who understood her ship like the mariners of old.

The night began to thicken until they were surrounded by blackness. Minnow dug her nails into the ship's wheel. This gloomy kind of dark was the stuff of her childhood nightmares. She tried not to think about the water beneath her and what it might hold, and instead kept singing, making her voice bright as a star.

Up ahead of her Raife was beaming. This was his favourite time. A breath between darkness and daylight, when the world was full of promise. He squinted through Mercy's antique binoculars, searching out a shoreline or far-off gleam of a summer mountain. But the night was cunning and had hidden even the stars.

He took his torch and thumbed again through the enchanting book, soon discovering there were plenty of stories that referenced Gatekeepers. A few that alluded to terrible storms where Gatekeepers were required to give something of themselves: a lock of their hair; a bone; three drops of blood. And in one case, a life.

'In rare moments between one Gatekeeper and another, the Gate remained closed and the Wild Deep was guarded by predators.'

He read softly. Minnow flinched. Raife moved his pocket torch further down the musty page.

'Simion, guardian of the Vintertide Gate, was over 500 years old. Fluorescent skin, eyes infected with hypnotic parasites, flesh poisonous to humans.'

Suddenly Raife began whooping like a wild gull. 'Minnow! I know what Simion is. He's the legendary Greenland shark!'

Minnow backed away in disbelief. 'It's a real thing? This shark?'

Raife couldn't get the words out fast enough. 'Yes. I mean like a thousand times yes. He's real. I've seen him. From afar. He's about 7 metres long and when he glows it's like . . . a miracle.'

Minnow stared Raife dead in the eye, but Raife was too excited to notice, and he began reeling off facts about his favourite deepwater hunter:

1) Greenland sharks were cannibals, growing huge teeth and killing their siblings in the womb, so only a single shark was ever born into the cold, grey, watery world at a time.

2) They were supposedly blind. Parasites and larvae formed their luminous eyelashes, which could hypnotize their prey.

3) Apart from teeth, they had no bones. They were an ever-moving skeleton made of muscle.

4) Their flesh was so potent that one bite could send you into a trance.

'And this man-eating monster is just swimming around near the Gate to Vintertide?' asked Minnow, trying to keep the fear out of her voice.

Raife nodded and Minnow looked ready to murder him. 'I can't just . . . swim into the jaws of a shark.' As Minnow spoke the words her nightmare loomed vividly around her. The starless sky. The inky sea. The dark where the beast lived waiting to hunt her. 'I can't do it,' she gasped, sitting down abruptly on the deck, the contents of her pocket digging sharply into her hip. With a skyward curse she pulled everything out, scattering a strange assortment of objects across the dark wood. A slither of moonlight glinted off Mercy's locket. Raife picked it up to give it back to her. As the locket passed between their hands it ever so gently rattled. They looked at each other. Miyuki padded over and put her wet nose to Minnow's cheek. The night leaned in closer. Carefully Minnow opened the locket and then whole world seemed to stop.

Inside were four small pointed teeth. Sharp like the spike of a sea urchin. So tiny they could have only belonged to a baby.

The wind seemed to still and the sea pressed in like a whispering wave. 'They must be yours,' Raife said after a long moment. Minnow rolled her eyes at him: 'Yeah, right.'

But Raife's face had become serious. 'You never keep still. You dived out of the water—not in. And you've got four silver teeth, where these ones must have once been.'

It seemed impossible to Minnow that those perfect, pixie-small teeth in the locket had come from her mouth and yet she knew, deep down, that they were hers.

The weird bones.

Sharks have skeletons made of cartilage.

The medication to help her sleep.

Sharks can never stop moving. Even in sleep they must swim to stay alive.

The way she could feel things in the air, like a person's thought or intention, even before it happened.

Sharks have eight senses.

And now these tiny shark teeth. As Minnow clasped the locket she felt as if a flame had lit the darkest part of her soul. 'You're right,' she breathed, 'I'm a . . . '

'You're the girl with the shark's teeth,' finished Raife, and the surf kissed the boat as if it agreed. They looked at each other in a way that neither of them had ever looked at anyone before. And perhaps never would again. Certainly they would both remember this moment for the rest of their lives, and whenever they encountered wonderful things, it would always be only a flicker of this same bright feeling.

'So?' asked Raife, sitting down and folding his arms. 'How would a girl with shark teeth cross the Wild Deep?'

Minnow imagined her mother, bold and untouchable, red hair flying in the wind. Beauty so fierce she could stare down a storm. 'She would cause a clever distraction. She would have a hook?'

Raife's face broke into a smile. 'I've got one!' He opened his rucksack, revealing a jumble of salt-worn fishing gear. 'We can distract the shark with some bait and you could swim . . . around him?' he suggested, sounding far more confident then he felt.

'All right,' said Minnow, looking anything but all right. 'Only I'm scared of the dark. I mean dark water.'

Raife rifled through his backpack and pulled out a small flare. 'This can be used underwater,' he explained. 'If the shark comes near you, this'll scare him off.'

Suddenly a dazzle of light out on the ocean cut through their vision. Minnow jumped and peered over the side of the boat. Beside her Miyuki gave a growl and Raife moved to the starboard side of *The Seafarer*. They had all seen it. But what was it? They waited in silence. The dark felt dense as a blanket, weighed down with the heaviness of a thousand unseen stars. Then it came again, brighter now, sweeping across the huge black boat and casting a ghostly shadow on the waves. And when the light was gone, through the Icelandic dark stood the faint silhouette of a lighthouse, as real as the rocks along the shore that can kill you.

'The lighthouse Lumière,' Minnow whispered.

Chapter Nine

THE LEGENDARY
GREENLAND SHARK

Minnow drew the huge boat up beside the strange drifting lighthouse. It was nothing like a lighthouse at all, since it wasn't stationary, or positioned on the rocks to warn sailors away from shore. Instead, it was floating in the middle of the ocean and built like a small chapel, with a tower so high that its circular beam resembled a slow-spinning star.

'If the lighthouse is floating, how do we know it's anywhere near the Vintertide Gate?' Minnow whispered.

'I guess we don't.' Raife lowered his voice and whispered in the knowledgeable way he had seen the older fisher folk do: 'Old Gunnar once told me it's anchored to the seabed, but drifts with the tide. So I suppose it's always near the Gate somehow; I mean that's how it's marked on the map. Let's drift, lower the bait, and wait. If the Greenland shark takes the bait, we're sure to know exactly where the Gate is and . . . '

Minnow nodded bravely. 'I can swim around him and enter the Wild Deep.'

'You can leave Miyuki and me at the lighthouse— when Arielka realizes we've gone she'll know exactly where to find me. But what about your boat?'

Raife had voiced the very thing Minnow had been silently fretting about this whole journey. Shakily, she tied one end of a diving rope around her waist and secured the other to the wooden mermaid figurehead.

'I'm going to pull the boat with me.' The words sounded crazy even to Minnow's ears.

Raife stared at her with such sharp, intense doubt, that Minnow couldn't meet his eye. 'Whatever you think,' said Raife numbly, as he unspooled a nylon halibut line and attached a wire hook he'd baited with seal blubber, looking at Minnow with disbelief.

'I'm a girl of the Wild Deep, and this is my ship. We belong together,' Minnow said, sounding more defiant than she felt.

What if something goes wrong? What if the Gate doesn't open and I'm stuck down there in the darkest part of the ocean?

Her gaze fell upon Miyuki and her heart went still. Leaving Miyuki would be hardest of all. The dog was an excellent sea swimmer, the best. But she was born of mountains and snowy peaks, untamed winds and winter stars. Not the crushing blackness of a lightless sea. For a moment Minnow struggled to breathe. A sob building in her throat. She closed her eyes to it, turning away as it burnt her. In a daze she climbed onto the lighthouse steps, Miyuki silently in step with her. The air was hurting her lungs, her feet were fighting to kick. She gave a pained gasp and dropped to her knees. 'No. No. I can't leave her . . .'

'A dog can't journey to the Wild Deep,' said Raife as gently as he could manage.

Minnow scowled at him so violently, that words tumbled out of Raife's mouth before he could stop them. 'Dogs aren't divers. She can't go that deep. She would drown in her own blood.'

Minnow went rigid with silence. 'You'll have to stay here girl,' she managed to stutter.

Miyuki gave a low accepting growl and Minnow laid her forehead against the husky's wolfish brow. And there they stayed, until Raife turned away, rubbing an invisible speck of salt that had slipped into his eye.

Somehow Minnow stood up. The dog didn't move, but sat obediently by the lighthouse steps. On leaden legs Minnow moved away. With each step the distance between them weighed on her, as if Miyuki was not just a dog but an anchor around which Minnow had drifted her entire life. To leave Miyuki was to be unmoored, untethered, and alone. She scrambled up onto the edge of *The Seafarer*, knowing that if she didn't do this quickly, she'd never do it at all. If the lighthouse Lumière marked the Vintertide Gate, then all they needed to do was find the shark and distract it so Minnow could swim through. *Sort of.*

At last the line pulled taut in Raife's hands, almost slicing his finger. Far below the surface something glimmered wickedly.

'That's the shark,' called Raife from the lighthouse.

'At least I'll know which direction I need to swim.' Minnow stood tall on the edge of her home, trying not to look at Miyuki and Raife waiting for her on the lighthouse steps. *I will find the Gate, and open it with a song.*

'The nylon line is 150 metres,' Raife said hurriedly.

'And the diving rope is about 250 metres,' Minnow answered, tightening it around her waist and double-checking it was knotted securely to the mermaid, bound round her waist, her throat, her fist and the curling fin of her wooden tail.

'If anything goes wrong before you hit 250 metres just tug on the nylon line. I'll jump onto the ship and pull you up,' said Raife nervously. Minnow smiled at him, a terribly sad little smile that made him suddenly doubt everything. He stood on the last step of the lighthouse and tried to hold Minnow's gaze.

'We don't have to do this. We could just go home and

wait for your mum there. Get hot chocolate and . . .'

Minnow shook her head. She thought of the men in the tunnel: the Sea Hunters. The gleaming scale around Jah Jah's neck. The bangle of hair round Ely's wrist. The velvet box of her mum's teeth. *This is the only way.*

'At least let me hold your trainers,' offered Raife.

'Nah,' replied Minnow, forcing herself to laugh brightly. 'Besides,' she grinned, flashing him a silver-cut smile, 'they're weighted!' And with that she dived.

A girl sleek as moonlight, arcing towards the sky, hitting the waves like an arrow. Her sequin Converse vanishing into the sea like swallowed stars. Raife could do nothing but stare, while Miyuki howled wildly beside him.

Water the colour of midnight enclosed Minnow's feet as she shot down, away from the guiding light of the moon. Away from the boat that was her home and her beloved Miyuki. Away from the green-eyed boy. Her heart racing in her chest, powering her on. The enormity of the task before her pushed to the farthest corners of her mind.

Find the Gate, open it with a song, pull the boat through, sail the Wild Deep. Easy.

Beneath the waves time and space were different. All of Minnow's worries faded away. She was weightless but full of wonder. Part salt water, part freedom. The rope around her was the only thing connecting her to the world above, its opposite end fastened to the beautiful black mermaid. Beside her somewhere in the deepening ocean was the nylon line, thin and tough as spider silk, reaching down to the jaws of the shark. In the greatness of the water it was almost invisible, but Minnow knew it was there, like a piece of the map that she could hold. *Stay away from the line*, she told herself. And yet she found herself circling towards it.

Soon Minnow was surrounded by deepest black. This was the dark she recognized from her nightmares, a cold bleakness that pulled her away from the world she knew. But still Minnow pressed on, ignoring the aching uncertainty that was spreading through her spine.

At around 120 metres deep, a terror suddenly hit her so sharply it seemed the water around her crackled. With a swift back curl Minnow slowed her dive, coming upright, or upside down, she wasn't sure. Everything felt wrong. The water was too thick, it was closing in and crushing her. She clung madly to the diving rope, desperate to pull it and signal for help. Her heart boomed in her ears like the tick of a bomb. *I want to go home. I don't like the dark.* Beside her the nylon fishing line pulled taut and all at once the swirling horror of her nightmares was real. She was lost in a lightless world and something was lurking below her. Something with teeth. Minnow could almost feel its thoughts.

A scream bubbled out of her throat, taking the last of her air. Minnow opened her mouth in shock and salt water rushed in. She was too deep to swim for the surface now, and too weak to pull on the rope. Her life would be taken by the unforgiving sea and she would never see her mama again.

Mama.

Confusion and dizziness blotted out all thought as Minnow felt a sharp pain on either side of her neck. She kicked out with the last of her energy as her silver scars expanded. Minnow felt the pressure ease as her open scars somehow took in life from the water. In the fierce cold sea she was breathing. *Breathing.* The oxygen calmed her. Stunned, Minnow put her hands to her neck. A slow realization swept over her. *They're not scars. They're gills.* And then she was dancing, twirling in the dark, weaving a watery show for the deep night ocean. For what delight could be more astounding than to breathe beneath the sea? *I am part shark. I am of the Wild Deep. I am Minnow.* She wanted to shout it to the ocean, but instead laughter spilled around her in a stream of musical bubbles. Minnow dipped and dived around, like a little fish touched with joy.

Then once again Minnow sensed the creature's presence below her and she curled into a ball, trying to feel where the shark was. But instead of pure fear, she felt the draw of something greater, something older and more magical. Its pull was like the magnetic draw of the north, only drawing her down instead of up. There was no way to stop it. There was no chance to turn back, she had to go to it, the same way an astronaut must go into the universe or a ballerina must enter the stage or a mountaineer must climb beyond the clouds. Minnow could feel the Gate calling to her. Only to reach the Gate, she would have to pass the shark.

The lightless ocean.
The unfathomable deep.
The watery creature that haunted her dreams.

Minnow realized something then. It was no good trying to swim around the shark. The shark was her beast, and she would have to face him. There was no other way.

Minnow reached out tenderly for the nylon line beside her, strong as spider silk. With a flicker of regret she kicked off her Converse, letting them float away. Then, with a single foot, Minnow felt for the thin blue line with her toes. There it was. She raised her arms like wings and slowly, slowly, one step at a time, she walked along the rope, threading it through her toes like a performer in an undersea circus, down and down.

One hundred steps later Minnow felt the smooth metallic arc of the hook. She had come to the end of the line. The shark had eaten the bait, which meant he was close. She curled herself around the hook and waited, eyes open, gradually adjusting to thick, deep dark.

Something moved ahead of her. There it was, at the edge of her vision, orbiting her. That movement. The circular curve of spine and fin. The swift, enclosing dread that her nightmares were made of. *The Beast*. Here he was, deathly beautiful and circling her, watching her with a pale unblinking eye, his mouth slightly open. His teeth the most heart-stopping thing Minnow had ever seen.

Nearer and nearer the creature came and still Minnow didn't move. She couldn't; she was mesmerized by the miracle of him. The poisonous flesh, the luminous larvae around his eyes. The way he softly glittered.

Ever so slowly the beast turned so he was swimming directly towards her. Minnow fumbled in her pocket for Raife's flare, but her fingers were clumsy with cold and it slipped from her grip, vanishing into blackness. The beast drew back its lips. Suddenly her skin felt as though it was on fire. She flailed in pain and confusion.

A long-lost memory broke to the surface of her mind. She was little, not yet able to walk and swimming out deep, her skin glowing underwater like a sunken star. Arielka's voice filled her mind: *In the deepest dark, you must be the light.* Minnow closed her eyes to the pain and let it rush in so it overtook every part of her. *I will be the light.* Her whole body seemed to sizzle, a burst of brightness broke over her skin. And then Minnow was glowing and gleaming. Open-mouthed, the shark came for her. But Minnow opened her eyes and swooped towards him, so they met nose to nose. Child to hunter.

From the steps of lighthouse Lumière Raife witnessed what he could only describe as an explosion of underwater stardust.

Miyuki started barking wildly. Raife turned away from the water to calm her and almost fell into the sea. In the window of the lighthouse was a face looking down at him, pale as the stars and both old and young all at once. He blinked and the face was gone. Raife backed away down the steps. *Was it a ghost? A water spirit?* He didn't know, but he suddenly had a fearful urge to get as far away from the lighthouse as possible. Without thinking, he climbed blindly onto *The Seafarer*, his heart hammering manically.

Far below Raife, the shark had swept away from Minnow, the gleam of her glowing skin so like a shark pup that he recognized her not as prey, but as kin. As a child of the Wild Deep. Minnow raced after him, the diving rope extending behind her till it was taut. Minnow's skin glowed like a shooting star; she felt an indescribable power surge through her. A speed and strength unrivalled.

And as Minnow dived deeper, she felt *The Seafarer* started to give way. Slowly the huge black ship above her started to tip, bow first, away from the night and the dawn and the world and slide into the water.

Raife panicked, fled to the galley and slammed the door. With the ship almost submerged it was too late for him to make it back onto the lighthouse steps. Frantically, Raife tied himself to a chair, nailed to the floor. The whole boat tilted until it was completely vertical. Raife cursed at the top of his lungs grabbing the sides of the chair. As the black ship hovered for a moment, Raife took a frenzied swig of air. Then the darkness rose, the ship went down, and the world disappeared.

Raife knew lots about free-diving. He understood the marvel of existing without oxygen—and how it could go wrong. But surely Minnow would save him? Surely it would not go wrong . . .

At three hundred feet below sea level everything alters, and the pressure rises to nine times what it is above water. Your heartbeat slows to a quarter of its rate. Your senses wash away and your reality becomes soft and dreamy.

At six hundred feet the pressure rises to eighteen times that on land. Your lungs shrink, and old amphibian instincts awaken. Raife knew that most humans would have had to turn back to the surface by now. As the boat flew at an impossible speed, with Raife still clinging on, a strange thought occurred to him: *What would happen to him beyond 250 metres?* But here in the dark depths of the unchangeable sea there was no place for doubt or worry. All Raife knew was there was something magical at work here and what ever happened next was unstoppable.

At that very moment the carved mermaid on the prow of the boat broke 250 metres and Raife felt a dreadful tightness in his chest, followed by a sharp pain on either side of his neck as the world closed in and he lost consciousness.

Suddenly, Minnow could see the Vintertide Gate up ahead. As she approached, an overwhelming sense of relief washed over her. As if this was the one gateway in all the world that she was supposed to go through. Not by jumping over, or wriggling beneath, but by opening with a lullaby to soothe bad dreams.

I am soul and song of water
I am fin and bone of star
I was dreamed from waves and moonlight
And my heart has swum so far.

'for the call of the sea starts when you're young
 And never stops chanting your name
Yes, the call of the sea starts when you're young
And never will you be the same.

'Oh, the sea it knows my secret
And the tides and winds they keep
Hidden from the wanderers far above
A place that's wild and deep.

'for the call of the sea, starts when you're young
And never stops chanting your name
Yes, the call of the sea starts when you're young
And never will you be the same.

I am cut from myth and marvel
I am scale and tooth and sea
I'll protect our ocean mysteries
If you'll only set me free.

'For the call of the sea starts when you're young
And never stops chanting your name
Yes, the call of the sea starts when you're young
And never will you be the same.

'Will soar towards the starlight
I will calm the surf with song
And if wanderers dare to follow
Their sweet lives will not last long.

'I am soul and song of water
I am fin and bone of star
I was dreamed from waves and moonlight
And my heart has swum so far.'

The shark coolly watched by Minnow's side as the ocean seemed to split in two, like a veil drawing back. Beyond the Gate, glittered a sea of silvery bright water. *The Wild Deep!* With a lasting glance at her shark—no longer a thing of nightmares, but a creature of ocean marvels—Minnow dived through the divide. The Gate seemed to sigh with recognition, then a ripping current whirled her into chaos, drawing the sea in behind Minnow, sweeping the black ship down after her and through the Gate . . .

The rope around Minnow's waist became twisted and Minnow struggled to swim on. She wondered if this had all been for nothing, if she would never see her mama again.

A single image floated to her. Miyuki stood on the steps of the lighthouse Lumière, blue eyes wild and searching, snout to the moon, heart beating for Minnow's return. And from somewhere deep inside her Minnow found the will to push and scramble gracelessly up towards the light.

She broke the surface of the water with a shriek, as wintry air hit her like a whip to the face. She had done it. She had made it into the Wild Deep! She barely had a second to take in the new world before *The Seafarer* came crashing up to the surface after her. The wind howled mercilessly but Minnow laughed through her shivering teeth. What a place of savage beauty the Wild Deep was.

Chapter Ten

THE WILD DEEP

Icebergs clustered around Minnow and frost burnt her throat. Everything was angel-wing white, and all she could do was tremble and stare.

Then with a delicate shimmer of air like rising smoke, Minnow's vision shifted and honed so that other colours emerged through the winter. Frozen emerald, frosted indigo, glacial gold. A seascape muted by cold. It was glorious. Violent shivers wracked through Minnow and she turned towards *The Seafarer*: back home. But as she came closer, through the galley porthole Minnow caught sight of a boy tied to her mum's chair. His green eyes were closed, head lolling to one side, body unmoving.

'No. No. No!' Her voice came out like cracking ice and she heaved up a lungful of seawater. *How could he be here?*

Minnow shot out of the water and onto the boat, ran over the icy deck and pounded on the galley door. 'Raife! Raife! You have to answer me.' She crashed to her knees, her adrenalin gone, her small body shaking with cold and shock. All she could do was call his name.

Seawater drained from the galley and the green-eyed boy spluttered awake. Raife stared around the sparse, damp room and wondered why it suddenly felt like Lapland. He untied himself quickly and stood up. Too fast. Droplets of scarlet blood scattered aimlessly from his nose and a painful ringing chimed in his ears. Raife flopped back down into the waterlogged chair, shivering as he waited for the dizziness to fade. In the space where there should have been silence, or softly whistling sea-wind, there came the sound of yelling. Raife stumbled to the door, as though walking through a dream, and heaved it open. There at his feet was a girl with a crown of frozen plaits, sobbing and calling his name.

In a gasp of icy air, the roar of the adventure came back to Raife.

He stayed on the boat by mistake.

Minnow had swum with the Greenland shark.

They had crossed through the Vintertide Gate into the Wild Deep.

'Minnow! You're alive! I'm alive! Everyone's alive!'

He dropped down and hugged the shaking girl. 'You did it,' he croaked, winter air scorching his throat. 'You opened the Gate . . . we're in the Wild Deep.'

Minnow gaped at the bedraggled, bloody-nosed boy before her. His hair was matted as straw, his eyes streaming with cold, his lips nearly blue. She had never been so grateful to see anybody in her entire life. 'What are you doing here?' she bellowed, her voice much angrier than she meant. 'You could have drowned. You could have died. I could have lost you . . . ' Minnow suddenly thought back to the moment when they'd first met. Raife had dived into the early morning sea as if the cold and the deep were nothing. 'How did you hold your breath for so long?' she asked more gently, but Raife only shrugged.

'Same way you did I guess,' he said before breaking into a coughing fit.

Minnow threw her arms around him, crying with relief. And Raife managed to wrestle them both inside, help Minnow struggle out of the diving rope and free the hook which was tangled in her hair.

'I didn't hold my breath,' Minnow panted, pointing at her scar-like gills. Raife stared at her in utter amazement. They were literally the coolest thing he'd ever seen.

'Maybe it was the Gate who saved us? Maybe it's magic?' Minnow murmured. 'Maybe the Gate grants a person life if they're brave enough to enter the Wild Deep?'

Raife gave a slow blink. 'Or maybe it's you. Maybe you saved my life; maybe you're the magic . . . ' Minnow wrinkled her nose, then another thought struck.

'Miyuki?' Minnow cried.

'I left her at the lighthouse, like we agreed,' said Raife a little sheepishly, but Minnow looked unexpectedly grateful.

'She'll swim to shore when the sun's up,' she smiled, and then: 'Water!'

Raife nodded, a terrible thirst suddenly upon him. He wrenched open the fridge, and—even though they both knew the rules about rationing things—they gulped down a huge bottle of water between them.

'What about your family?' asked Minnow. 'Won't they be worried?'

Raife looked nonplussed. 'Mum's opening a new exhibition and my stepdad Viktor's just got a new bicycle, and they'll probably just think I'm at fish camp. Unless Mad Elka—I mean, unless Arielka tells them I'm here.'

Minnow grimaced, thinking how angry her grandmother would be when she discovered Minnow and the book were gone, but there was no time to worry about that now. They were shivering half to death and on the cusp of a great adventure.

Raife rubbed the dried blood off the end of his nose with the sleeve of his parka. Minnow wrenched open a watertight chest and pulled out some spare clothes.

Raife showed her how to dress for the cold in a series of layers: wintertime was no match for an Icelander. All you needed was the right jumper. (Or the right number of vests, t-shirts and sweaters.) Together they stared at the whaleskin map, marvelling at the fact that they were really about to cross the Wild Deep.

'We're in Vintertide and we'll have to go through Darkentide to reach Somertide.'

Minnow nodded dreamily. 'So roughly a day in each tide?'

'Depends,' Raife said, 'how fast we travel and who we meet along the way.'

They both stared at each other brightly, their minds glittering with the same swift thought. *Will we really meet a mermaid?*

'Right then,' said Minnow, once they were finally warm. 'Let's explore!'

She threw the galley door open and stepped into ankle-deep snow. At once Minnow felt a tension lift from her limbs as it did beneath the waves. The air was easier to breathe here and everything felt clearer, like the sharpening into focus of a kaleidoscope. *So, this is the Wild Deep*, she thought, and then, *Is this where I belong?*

Beside her Raife saw only whiteness, infinite and dazzling. Then he blinked and shielded his eyes, experiencing the same splitting of vision Minnow had as the real colours of the world broke through. 'I can hear a horse,' he said after a moment. They were miles from land. Minnow spun around and gave an inward gasp as a herd of wild horses came galloping over a mound of lilac snow and plunged into the sea, moving with the menacing grace of orcas, banking on a sea-green iceberg and galloping off into the misty distance.

A word hung in Raife's mind: 'Seahorses.'

'Just look at the boat,' Minnow laughed, kicking up a flurry of snow. Ice crystals had covered every sail and snow constellations decorated every beam, each surface gilded with winter, so *The Seafarer* looked like a ship cut from diamonds. Raife gave a merry laugh and unwound a sail, admiring its snowy sheen. Then he dropped the sail and almost swallowed his heart. On a lump of ice, not more than 6 metres away lounged a colony of polar bears. Huge, wild, feral hunters.

Minnow followed Raife's gaze and on seeing the bears, dropped soundlessly onto her knees and crawled across the deck, shoving him lightly behind the open sail. A light wind whispered, or perhaps it was Raife trembling? Either way Minnow noticed a patch of fabric on the sail just above their heads that was worn thin by sea-winds. She balanced on her toes and peered through, almost letting out a cry of laughter. She clapped a hand over her mouth and motioned to Raife to peek through.

The bears were settled on old oil barrels that had frozen into the landscape in a misshapen circle. Their majestic heads turned towards each other. Were they playing a game of cards? Maybe poker? A large red-eyed bear with a scarred nose grunted as she laid down her hand. Her comrades responded with guttural, low snorts that came to Minnow and Raife's ears like a lullaby sung by drunken bandits.

'It sounds like Old Norse,' Raife mouthed. 'They are speaking the language of fairy tales.' And even though they were both a little terrified of these huge sovereigns of winter, they couldn't keep from smiling.

When they had drifted on a safe distance from the polar bears, Minnow began readying the boat for the journey: tightening ropes and shaking snow from the rigging, eager to get moving.

Raife laid the whaleskin map down in the snow, figuring out their best route. 'Strange that we haven't seen any of the mystical folk of the Deep yet . . . '

Just then, a different sound floated by and Minnow and Raife stiffened. Voices. Unmistakably human. Raife stuffed the map in his pocket and Minnow pulled him swiftly back behind the sail. Glancing through the gap they saw another boat bobbing into view. Though it wasn't quite like any boat Minnow had seen before. Its hull was crafted from the body of a maroon Skoda truck, and its sail was cut from the Scottish flag. It had three men inside. And it was followed by an array of strange handcrafted sea-carriers. There was a vessel made from a big metal bin chopped in half, a sail fashioned from a pink beach mat. A Vietnamese woven bamboo basket, crammed with people using mop handles like a paddle. There was a slow-drifting bathtub, rowed by a woman with glittering skin using sheaves of lavender, and an oak bed and mattress, on which someone—or something—was sleeping. There was a wheelbarrow boat, an entire garden shed nailed to two surfboards, a shining cello with a sunshade sail, and a fleet of floating plant pots, each holding a single small passenger.

'It's like a carnival on water,' said Minnow, utterly charmed by the flotilla.

Raife wasn't so sure. The sea-carriers had all been built with a rough defiant skill, and decorated with seaweed and sculpted icicles, but there was a sense of purpose to them. As though they might have been readying themselves for a fight. And the flotilla was directly blocking their course.

A shouted greeting came across the water, straight from the Skoda-float. A note of intimidation seemed to beat the air. Minnow and Raife stared at each other in tight-lipped horror.

'They can't see us here,' Minnow hissed, knowing her own boat from every angle. 'There are three sailors.' Minnow squinted through the sail. 'Seriously, Raife— you've got to see them. They've got beards beyond any fisherman's wildest dreams.'

Raife wriggled his face in close and was not disappointed. The beards were green as kelp, tangled with barnacles and so spectacularly long, that the men had draped them around themselves like sashes of honour. The way the grey light fell across their skin made them dazzling. It was hard to look at them directly.

'They're iridescent,' murmured Minnow.

'We need to get out of the way, and sail around the flotilla,' said Raife anxiously. 'I'll keep the boat steady and you control the wind with your song.'

Minnow glanced at him doubtfully but Raife didn't hesitate. He stepped out from behind the sail with an easy confidence and took up the wheel. 'Just look busy and don't make eye contact,' he hissed.

Minnow took a lungful of crisp air and raced up the rigging. She had no idea whether she should sing her lullaby or something else. Minnow closed her eyes feeling the mood of the day, the strange sight of the flotilla and the dancing snowfall. It reminded her of Reykjavik in winter. So she sang an Icelandic nursery rhyme Arielka had taught her. It was an offbeat choice but it seemed fitting to her somehow.

Sleep now, black-eyed pig, fall into a pit of ghosts . . .

There was a breath of wind in the sails. Raife shot Minnow a quick look: *Keep singing.* As Minnow sang and Raife steered, the boat began to turn, moving out of the wide green waterway into a smaller rivulet that curled away to somewhere quieter, leaving the flotilla behind.

'Check the map and see if you recognize anything,' called Minnow.

But Raife was staring hard at something afloat on the water. Minnow followed his gaze and felt herself sicken. There in the frozen sea was a girl as white as winter, lying flat just beneath the surface, her eyes closed as if in sleep.

In a single bound Minnow was up on the edge of the boat, knees bent, hands raised in the perfect point of an arrow. But as she hovered on the brink of the brackish sea something stopped her. A pulse glimmered beneath her, like the powerful pound of a heart. Just as she'd sensed the shark, Minnow became vividly aware of the girl's life force and her dark, crackling intention.

'What's wrong?' Raife demanded, as Minnow toppled back onto the deck.

'It's a trap,' she breathed, grabbing Raife's arm to pull him back.

But even though all those years fishing with Old Gunnar had taught Raife to be cautious, he couldn't just leave this girl in the sea to drown. He shoved Minnow aside, rubbing his arm furiously and barking, 'I'm sorry,' as he jumped over the side of the boat.

Minnow flew after him, catching his shin moments before he hit the water. He was so much heavier than she'd expected. Even with a life of raising anchors the weight of him knocked her breath from her. She braced herself against the side of the boat, leaning back like a windsurfer on the cusp of a storm. And there the green-eyed boy hung, hovering above the floating girl like the prince in *Sleeping Beauty* moments before the kiss. There was only the salty sea between them. Raife reached down to lift her from the water, and the girl's eyes flashed open. Flat and pink they gleamed at him perilously. With a terrible gloat she seized Raife's wrists and pulled him down towards a watery grave.

Chapter Eleven

LIGHT FINS

Minnow skidded backwards, Raife's blue hi-top coming off in her hands. *I can't let Raife die now!* she thought, casting the shoe aside and diving after him. *Especially not with only one trainer.* As she arced into the water something clicked within her, and everything was fluid, she was movement and melody and muscular grace, and nothing would stop her.

But the vicious girl was equally fast and Raife was her prisoner: a boy who had studied sharks of every variety; a boy who loved the sea from the moment he first heard its call; a boy who envied the seafarers of old who had lost their ships to phantom white whales. Even though dizziness was setting in, Raife would not go down without a fight. He squeezed his eyes shut and made a fist, then someone was grabbing his foot, trying to steal his other trainer. *The injustice of it!*

He glanced upwards, but instead of an enemy saw a girl with dancing plaits, and burning bright skin and he accidentally smiled, letting out his last breath of oxygen. Then with an act of sheer willpower Minnow pulled Raife and the girl back up to the surface, a twirling torpedo of bodies. Minnow hauled them all up and they slid across *The Seafarer*'s deck with a sickening thud.

'Thank you,' Raife whispered to Minnow as he broke free of the vicious girl and began vomiting on the deck. Minnow scowled crossly, and then immediately leapt up, ready to fight. The vicious girl rose up with a slickness smooth as water. As Minnow took in the very strangeness of her, she suddenly realized exactly what the girl was. *She's a Light Fin!* A creature from one of her bedtime stories. *It's all real*, thought Minnow. *Every single tale of the sea is real.*

The girl's skin was pale as ice, her teeth amphibian-like, not shark but something smaller. *Maybe a water-snake?* Her hair was the blue of midnight ice caps, yet the most startling thing about her was that protruding through the back of her faded t-shirt were two ethereal wing-size fins that gave her the rare grace of a fairy.

'All right—you win!' she said in Finnish.

Wow, they play rough here, thought Raife, still trying to catch his breath.

'We win. Yay us,' he answered in Icelandic, hoping to every Nordic god he could name she would understand.

To his surprise the girl chuckled, a delighted little laugh that rang out like a bell.

'I love your sea-soul,' she continued, running her hands over *The Seafarer*'s sails as if they were cut from the cloth of heaven. It took Raife and Minnow a moment to realize that sea-soul meant boat.

'Oh, thanks,' mumbled Raife, mistakenly switching to English.

Luckily the Light Fin did the same. 'You must be from Darkentide; we don't have sea-souls like this around here; we tend to craft our own. It's beautiful.'

'It's mine,' said Minnow, suddenly feeling protective.

The Light Fin eyed Minnow curiously, and Minnow realized how odd they must look. A pasty, gagging boy, and a brown girl with silver teeth.

'You're pretty far from the regatta.'

So that's what the flotilla of boats was: *A regatta*. A party of some kind.

'What are you doing so close to the edge?'

'The edge of what?' asked Raife, hoping the girl wouldn't judge them. She seemed mostly OK, almost sweet, despite having nearly drowned him.

'The edge of the Deep!'

The edge of the world, thought Minnow, recalling how explorers of old believed the world to be flat. How they feared sailing over the 'edge' like a wall of water: *A waterfall beneath the waves.* Was this where sunken ships of the world ended up? Where history met with marvel?

The Light Fin eyed them both curiously. 'You know you two could definitely pass.'

Raife remembered a line from a story in the fairy tale book. *In the Wild Deep a creature more human than fish could sometimes pass between the worlds.*

Minnow nodded. 'Yeah—thanks.'

'What bloodline are you?' The Light Fin's eyes narrowed.

Minnow felt a jolt of panic. *What Am I?* Her teeth began to pain her, startling the answer from her lips. 'I'm a shark-tooth.'

The name stirred something in Minnow's bones. *I'm a shark-tooth.* It felt powerful and purposeful, yet it brought Minnow a sense of peace.

Raife grinned at her a little manically, and his excitement made Minnow want to laugh.

'Let's go inside the galley,' Minnow offered, trying to steer the conversation away from her. Raife quickly lit the lanterns and the galley filled with the scent of salt and sea-herbs. Minnow boiled the kettle and the Light Fin went wild with excitement, examining the starfish paperweight, peering keenly at the plants, and staring mutely at the humming fridge.

'I'm Minnow, what's your name?' Minnow asked, trying to distract the pink-eyed creature from the items in the galley which were clearly from the Far Above.

'Fairlith,' the Light Fin answered in her sing-song voice.

Minnow handed Fairlith one of Mercy's finest china teacups. Fairlith cradled the cup as if it were magical. 'Where did you get this beautiful thing? Is it carved from bone?'

Minnow and Raife glanced at each other nervously, both willing the other not to let the truth slip. Something told them that letting Fairlith know they were from the Far Above would be dangerous.

They were rescued by a high-pitched note. Fairlith discarded the teacup and dashed onto the deck. 'That's my cousin Fern-Rae!' she squealed.

Outside another Light Fin was lounging on the ice floe as if it were a bath of warm milk. Fern-Rae swam over and slunk up onto *The Seafarer* with an eel-like ease, settling herself on the side and casually crossing her long legs. There was an aura about her that made Minnow feel like bolting, but she pushed her feet into the snow and stayed grounded. The older Light Fin had long plum-coloured hair, eyes of fishscale grey and, unlike her cousin, perfectly human teeth. The only thing which drew the eye was a single line of transparent fins along the back of her arms and legs.

'Hi,' she grinned, but the smile was cold.

There was something menacing about Fern-Rae, which Raife didn't like. He'd grown up in a small community where newcomers were often treated with suspicion. So he made his expression as distant and aloof as Fern-Rae's was, knowing they had to imitate her behaviour to fit in.

But Minnow had grown up on a boat at the edge of a colourful city, with a mother who welcomed everyone (when she wasn't fighting them). Minnow had lived her whole life with the quiet chaos of not-quite-belonging, and got through it by smiling over her fears. She beamed at the older Light Fin with her wildest, silver-struck grin.

At once Fern-Rae advanced towards Minnow. It wasn't quite walking, but more like sliding while standing at the same time. It was both amazing and quite awful to watch. 'Your teeth,' she said, 'they're silver?'

Minnow closed her mouth, her cheeks turning pink. She could sense the doubt rising up in the older girl like a mist. *Who are you?*

Raife, Minnow, Fairlith, and Fern-Rae stared at one another and silence fell upon the boat.

'You're a shark-tooth. What's happened to your mouth? Did someone make you take out your shark teeth?' Fairlith breathed, dismayed.

'No. No—no one made me,' Minnow said hurriedly. 'I chose it. As a dare. No one believed I'd do it, but guess what? I did.'

The two Light Fins looked utterly appalled. They

began retreating, with a movement that made Minnow think of snakes.

'Look, it was actually part of her training,' improvized Raife.

Fern-Rae stilled. 'Training?'

Raife gave a nonchalant shrug. 'Yeah. Minnow's training to be a Gatekeeper—thought that was obvious.'

Yes! thought Minnow, quite giddy with the perfection of Raife's lie.

Fern-Rae looked mightily surprised, whilst Fairlith went into a sort of shrieking fit of joy, leaping around the boat, calling out gleefully, 'Are they really training folk in Darkentide . . . We thought everyone had lost hope. Are you actually training to be a Gatekeeper?'

Minnow gave a defiant nod.

'So the Gate will really open? I mean it never has in my lifetime, but maybe the Merfins were right. Maybe the curse really will lift and the Gate will choose another,' Fairlith said, in a rush.

Fern-Rae flicked her long lilac hair off her slim shoulders and spat over the side of the boat. 'I doubt it,' she said, catching her cousin sharply by the arm. 'The Gate has been locked for twelve years and it might not ever open unless the Betrayer returns or the Gate chooses another Keeper.'

Minnow felt an uncomfortable twitch at the word Betrayer, and though she tried to ignore it and keep grinning, Raife's lie suddenly felt fragile, as if it might dissolve at any moment. There was so much about the Wild Deep they didn't know.

'Good luck with your crazy training,' said Fern-Rae icily. Fairlith gave them one last demonic grin and then the Light Fins melted over the side of the boat and disappeared beneath the waves without so much as a splash.

Minnow's heart was fluttering like a diving swallow. 'They don't believe us,' she gasped, panic welling up in her.

'I know,' said Raife. 'I think it was my trainers that gave us away.'

Minnow scowled at him, but then she kind of realized Raife actually had a point. 'You're right—we need to find a way to blend in. If they find out we came from the Far Above and passed through the Gate, who knows what they'll do with us.' And with that she bundled Raife into the galley and began unbinding Mercy's huge box of costumes.

Ten minutes later Minnow and Raife were staring at each other in the galley's long mirror. They had wriggled out of their layers of t-shirts, leaving on light vests, and hacked Raife's jeans off at the knee with kitchen scissors. On the back pocket of her shorts Minnow had sewn a beautifully embroidered compass, sliced straight out of an atlas of silk from the map cupboard. Then she'd slipped on her mum's purple gypsy top and fastened a musty leather waistcoat over the top, adorned with real peacock feathers, which she'd pulled from a hat and stapled on. Over each of the waistcoat pockets she'd stuck a small, dried sea aster, using a watertight sealant from Mercy's desk. Then she'd torn a sequin scarf for them to wear as matching bandanas. The effect was quite wonderful.

Raife had thrown on an orange tie-dye t-shirt of Mercy's and he'd stitched a map in the shape of an albatross onto the back, feathers and all. Over this he'd fixed a gold, bullet-studded belt-turned-sash. They'd both painted their nails in blood red, and marked their cheeks with black lipstick, a bit like rugby players. But the best thing of all was that Raife had customized Mercy's sleep mask, creating a fantastic magenta eyepatch, which he now wore over one eye.

'Can you even see with that on?' Minnow cackled, falling to the floor in a fit of giggles.

'Not really,' Raife admitted. 'It's a bit like when you have an eye test. Only worse because we're at sea.'

'Take it off!' Minnow bellowed with laughter.

'Nah. It makes me look interesting.'

Minnow sat up, wiping happy tears from her cheeks. 'But you are already interesting.'

Raife stared at her with his one visible eye. 'No I'm

not,' he said matter-of-factly.

'You know loads about fishing, tons about the sea, and absolutely everything about sharks, and you can even read Old Norse.'

'Most people think that stuff is boring.'

Minnow glared at him. 'Well not me. I love sharks . . .'

Raife chuckled. 'Yeah, well, that's because you are one.'

They stumbled out onto the deck, Minnow roaring with laughter every time Raife stubbed his toe, or almost walked into the mast. Outside the light was changing, shifting to a luminous version of dusk. At once a gleeful hush fell over them. Raife readjusted the magenta eyepatch so it now sat over his bandana, then scooted up the rigging to the crow's nest to keep watch for any passing ships—or sea-souls as they now knew they were called. It was time to get back on course.

Time to sail across the Wild Deep and rescue Mama. Minnow moved to the centre of the deck and focused her energy, feeling the lilt of the breeze on her neck, listening to the gentle splash of the sea, tasting the sweetness of snowflakes. Minnow was beginning to understand the power of her song, so she took a deep, ocean-bound breath and with all her wild shark heart sang the first sea shanty that came into her head.

'Down by the shore of the night deep sea
A child was singing so prettily.
She kicked and she laughed in the moon-bright waves
Yet nobody saw her fearless and brave.

'But the sea eyed the child,
And the sea understood.
For a land of Wanderers,
This child was too good.

'The sea raised her tide
And took the child down.
Gifted her gills,
So she couldn't ever drown.

'Swept her out far,
Through the Gate of silver-blue
To the Wild Deep ocean
Where she could be true.'

It was a ditty Mercy had taught her. Somehow

singing it made Minnow feel closer to her mum, as if the words were an enchantment that might draw them back together.

A merry little gale whirled through the sails, tugging the boat playfully into the rivulet of blue ice. Just for a moment Minnow thought she saw a figure drifting spectre-like across the waves, but as she gazed at it, it melted back into a flurry of snow.

As they glided into the thickening dusk, the snow vanished, and storm-beaten patches of forest sprouted out of the ice. They were nearing Darkentide. Around them winter woods had grown at odd angles. The roots of the trees were still encased in ice, so each berg was in fact a floating islet. Peering through Mercy's binoculars Raife spotted a hotchpotch of homes nestled between the trees. Little communities that clung to the ice, like barnacles to a rock. Yet the homes themselves were empty. *Perhaps they all went to the regatta*, he thought.

The loneliness of the place went straight to Minnow's heart. There was something about the little abandoned homes that touched her. This was not the Wild Deep she had heard of in stories, this place felt shadowed in sorrow, a sense of struggle clinging to the air. Beached rowing boats had been turned upside down to make camps. A faded blue sail was a tent. Two oars and a stained, floral tablecloth tied to make a wigwam. But there was no comfort, only a cold sense of despair.

Minnow could only wonder at why, but she had no answers. Yet as she sang about the Gate of silver-blue she began to think about what the Light Fins had said: 'The Gate has never opened in my lifetime . . .' *Why not?*

Behind Minnow, Raife fell still. The eeriness reminded him of the graveyard of boats, only it felt as though these boats were awake and watching them sail past.

A loud chiming from below cut through Minnow's song. 'The clock!' she cried. It hadn't chimed since Minnow was lost in the fog, so why was it chiming all of a sudden now? They both dashed through the galley and into Mercy's cabin. The clock doors below the star of the north burst open and a small carved orca popped out on a spring.

'I keep forgetting it can do that,' Minnow panted. 'Last time it chimed, a swallow dived out.'

Raife stepped closer to examine the ornate model. It was so flawlessly made, even the paintwork seemed to gleam, as if the whale was deep underwater. 'It's beautiful—'

The whole boat suddenly pitched violently to the side as if nudged from below.

Minnow and Raife caught one another's hands.

'What's going on?' whispered Raife. But before Minnow could speak there was another bump which sent the boat back the other way.

'Is something . . . knocking on the boat?' But even as

Minnow spoke these words, understanding was dawning on her face and Minnow was on her feet, dancing out the door and up the stairs. 'Whales,' came her voice drifting down to Raife. He stared at the tiny model orca, and the grandeur of the clock. And he wondered if there was more to this clock than met the eye.

Raife was right to wonder, because the clock was not simply telling them the time. It was warning them of what was to come. For as Raife stepped onto the deck, he saw that glimmering below in a twisting storm of snouts and tails, was not just one but a pack of strikingly magnificent killer whales.

The largest one raised its tail as though in greeting and Minnow and Raife found themselves open-mouthed in awe.

'I think they want you to follow,' said Raife. 'There's an awful lot of them.'

Minnow was mesmerized. For the whales, killer or not, were summoning her. It was not a call she could ignore.

'Have we got time for this? I mean shouldn't we be sailing across the Wild Deep to rescue Mercy, not swimming with cold-hearted killers?' Raife asked a little nervously, but Minnow acted as if she could hardly hear him, as if she'd already fallen under the whales' spell.

Thinking quickly, Raife darted inside the galley and returned with the half tangled length of nylon halibut line—he unclipped the hook from the end of it and handed it to Minnow. 'Just in case,' he said as she tucked the hook through the belt-loop of her shorts. Then he fiddled and tugged and tweaked the line until it unspooled like a length of unspun cobweb. 'Here we go,' Raife said, tying one end around Minnow's left ankle and the other around his own so they were bound together. So no matter where Minnow was drawn to, Raife could eventually follow. Or if something in the Wild Deep separated them, they would always be able to find each other. 'If you need help . . . If anything—'

'I know!' Minnow snapped. 'Three sharp tugs.'

Raife frowned at her. 'One tug. And I'll dive in.'

Minnow wasn't listening. The whales were calling and Raife's voice was blocking their song. She pushed him carelessly out of the way, not looking back as she sprang gloriously into the air, gliding into the sea, smooth as silk. A girl among a squall of killers. The green-eyed boy forgotten.

Chapter Twelve

A SHARK AMONG ORCAS

Minnow shot into the herd of inky-skinned beasts as if she were their queen, her own skin fizzing gold like a sea-star. The orcas formed a circle around her, a loop of fins and tails and eyes that watched her with a quiet, killer wisdom and down they all went. A pack of feral dreamers. Minnow felt special, gifted, and honoured. There was something so deeply reassuring about swimming with the whales, that on impulse she reached out and touched a smooth snout. A wise eye blinked at her. It felt like an invitation, and Minnow accepted, leaning in and resting her body against the orca's smooth back, putting her ear to its fin, her arms around it in a half hug. It was the loveliest sensation in all the world. And in the starry-dark below the sea Minnow found herself crying. For all that she was, for all that she'd been, for all that perhaps she could be, in the twisting tides of the *Wild Deep*.

An ache of regret tugged at her heart. *All those years on land feeling lost. Why did Mama never bring me here? Never explain to me where I come from?* Her grandmother's clipped voice answered from a memory: *Gatekeepers can never have children.* Minnow bit her lip, holding in a sob. *Perhaps I don't belong in either place*, she thought sadly. *Or maybe I belong in both.* And she knew, in her bones that this was right. She was a girl of two worlds. Part black, part white; part human, part shark; part Far Above, part Wild Deep. And that was the brightest magic Minnow had ever known.

On *The Seafarer*, Raife was alone in the deepening dusk, the nylon line very slowly trailing into the sea. He knew it would be best to keep busy and not to count the minutes until Minnow's return. *I'll pretend I'm night fishing*, he decided. And then, *Is fishing even allowed in the Wild Deep?* On a sea that was home to many long-forgotten and unknown sea-creatures maybe fishing wasn't the done thing. So he settled for star-gazing instead. It was something he and Old Gunnar had spent hours doing in the stillness of pre-dawn mornings and it held its own timeless magic.

Raife was quietly delighted to find the stars in the Wild Deep were different. So much further away, and many more of them, each twinkling with a hint of colour like the final moments of a firework. Soon the sea was aglow with reflections, so Raife felt as if he was moored upon a lake of floating jewels. He didn't hear the clouds stirring with wingbeats.

When Minnow thought they could go no deeper, a fern forest loomed below. It was lit with the glow of sea snails and the spangle of starfish, like a field of rushes on the seabed. The whale gave a shimmer of oily skin and Minnow slid off his back and into a thicket of kelp. Gently the whale nudged Minnow's shoulder and she began to walk into the undersea forest. *They're protecting me*, she thought, though her fingers still reached for the base of the hook.

A pulse brightened the water. Minnow turned, already knowing what she would find. There in the heart of the kelp was a familiar figure. One with snowy skin and hair the colour of ice caps in the moonlight. Two wing-shaped fins shimmering behind her: *Fairlith*. For a moment neither Minnow nor the Light Fin moved. They eyed one another suspiciously. A ring of whales looped around them, so the space in between became their own little planet.

Up on the deck of *The Seafarer* Raife suddenly spoke out loud. 'Orcas hunt sharks,' said Raife out loud on the deck of *The Seafarer.* He'd suddenly remembered a clip he'd watched one rainy lunchtime at school. 'They flip great whites onto their backs, so the shark can't fight back. Then they strike.' He felt sick to the bottom of his gut. He grabbed the halibut line, and got ready to haul Minnow back in. Who knew how deep she was? He tried desperately not to think about the image of her vanishing amongst a pod of shark-killing hunters, bile rising in his throat.

Then there was a shuffling of dark air, a swooping of wings, and footfall on the deck behind him. Ever so slowly Raife turned his head. His heart went still with shock. Two almost-boys stood at the stern of the ship. They were the exact opposite of each other. One white as a ghost and the other black as night; both had a pair of huge, imposing wings. The white-skinned boy had the midnight wings of a raven and the black-skinned boy had the white wings of a snowy owl. Apart from the wings and downy feathers that lined their heads, they were otherwise human. Mostly. For there was also a beakiness about their noses, and a beady-eyed quality to them, which reminded Raife of an eagle.

Raife should have run or dived into the water, but he found he could do nothing but stare. Because they were terrifying and beautiful all at the same time.

'But I want wings!' Raife cried, startling the boys on deck but most of all himself. He couldn't swear to it, but as the boys hoisted him unsteadily into the air he thought one of them gave him an apologetic shrug. Then Raife was yelling in horror, as they flew in the most wonky, bumpy, unstable manner imaginable into the night sky. He found himself grabbing at handfuls of feathers to save himself from crashing to his death. To worsen Raife's plight the bird-boys started having an argument in French over the top of his head. Their beaky noses repeatedly jabbed him on the head. As Raife rose higher, the nylon line unravelled, until at 10 metres in the air it pulled taut and he was stuck.

In the kelp forest Fairlith took a single floating step closer to Minnow, her expression sad and guarded. 'Who are you?' she asked, her voice coming out like an echo. Minnow gathered her thoughts and sent them out like a beam of words travelling through the long reeds. To her surprise it was easy.

'I am Minnow,' she said, trying to sound important. She felt a pain in her ankle. Someone, or something, was tugging on the line. She looked down and suddenly remembered. Raife. But they weren't that deep down— the line was 150 metres . . . Why would Raife be pulling her up?

The orcas began to close in. *It's a trap,* Minnow thought. *They led me away from the boat. Now they're going to kill me.*

Minnow's hands clasped the hook and she stabbed blindly in front of her, kicking harder than ever as she shot towards the surface, helped by the nylon line which was dragging her up like a fish in a net.

The black whales swarmed after her, hungry for the chase, but Minnow didn't care. Her adrenalin had awoken within her. Below her Fairlith shouted something frenzied up to Minnow but she didn't hear.

The nearer the killer whales came, the faster she zoomed, the distance between them only stretching. Out of the star-bright sea Minnow tore, a roar of wrathful shout breaking from her lips. She managed to land on *The Seafarer's* deck, skidding unstoppably across the boat from starboard to port, turning her fall into a clumsy cartwheel. As she spun upside down Minnow followed the line attached to her ankle up into the sky. Raife was somehow in the air, being pulled away by human birds. Fern-Rae and a gang of other sea-kids were suddenly skimming up out of the water and onto *The Seafarer.* They were the strangest, yet most wonderful collection of sea-folk Minnow had ever seen. Some had electric light crackling from their fins. Others had scaled skin, hard as armour. One had stingray fins that fell about him like a cape. But there was a terrible sense of menace from all of them. Minnow remembered how envious Fairlith was of *The Seafarer*—her sea-soul. Had they come to take it?

Minnow's home was under attack and her best friend was being kidnapped. There was nothing else for it—gritting her teeth, Minnow dived over the port side of the boat, dipping beneath it, zipping in and out of the waiting orcas, punching the snout of any beast who came for her. The agony in her ankle was almost unbearable, as the nylon line stretched taut, slowly pulling Raife and the bird-boys back down. Using a propeller spin, Minnow twirled back onto the boat, pelting across the deck, before shooting back into the sea. This time she surfaced at the stern of her home and ran along the deck, dodging the swiping hands of the sea-kids and coming up starboard, pulling the line tauter still and binding both her and Raife to the boat. Raife, still clasped 10 metres in the air by the trembling bird-boys, could go no higher, and no one could steal *The Seafarer* without facing Minnow first.

She stood with her back to the galley door, heart beating, fists raised. The mob of sea-kids perched, lounged, or hung over every part of the boat.

'Get off my sea-soul,' Minnow's voice came out high and clear. Nobody moved. Somebody sniggered. Minnow's hands found the hook. 'I said get off!' She ran at them, brandishing the hook like a sword.

They lunged back at Minnow. For a moment she was slightly restricted by the line still linking her to the boat and to Raife. But with a sharp kick it extended further, so Minnow could move freely whilst bound to her beloved home. She was so angry, and more than that, she was afraid. It was the kind of fear that made you feel invincible, like a boxer entering a ring or a skier at the sheerest point of a mountain. Twice, three times Minnow was pinned to the deck by scaled, sinister hands. Every time she wriggled free. A tempest with a piece of deadly silver.

The bird-boys hovered above, staring at the spectacular scene unfolding on the deck. From his vantage point in the sky, Raife—without thinking—started cheering for Minnow. There was a flap of forlorn feathers, and a lot of swearing in French as one of the bird-boys mistakenly let go for a moment and then suddenly Raife was free, falling through the sky.

Chapter Thirteen

THE HIGH WINDS

Terror seized Raife's heart. The bird-boys swooped after him.

While Minnow was momentarily distracted, the sea-kids saw their chance and attacked. In a single, collective move Minnow was slammed to the floor, her loose silver tooth knocked clean from her mouth. Her limbs were pinned down and her own fishing hook held to her throat.

The bird-boys burst into their own strange song; Minnow was startled to see that they too could summon the winds, and Raife's fall slowed until he was lowered to the deck in the soft embrace of evening. Then all of a sudden the peaceful feeling was gone and Raife found himself tangled in the rigging. The bird-boys crashed roughly into him, as they misjudged their own landings.

Minnow gave a shudder of relief to see that Raife was

safe. Fern-Rae gave a shriek of hot fury. She released the hook from Minnow's neck and started shouting a torrent of abuse at the bird-boys in Old Norse. They hung their wings in shame, shuffling backwards in a way that reminded Minnow of two nervous penguins. Raife, who was now caught between the bird-boys, started to feel quite sorry for them. Fern-Rae seemed so appalled with the winged pair for dropping Raife and ruining the kidnap plan, that Raife began to fear for all three of them.

But during his sky-borne adventure Raife had to come to realize that the winds of the Wild Deep could be used for many things and if they could shift a great ship, or catch a falling boy, perhaps it could even stop a murderous Light Fin? As Fern-Rae whipped towards them, a storm of purple hair, Raife took a deep and uncertain breath and, hoping with everything he had that the bird-boys might join him, he began to sing Minnow's lullaby.

'I am soul and song of water
I am fin and bone of star
I was dreamed from waves and moonlight
And my heart has swum so far.'

There was a small beat of silence. Raife gazed at the bird-boys pleadingly, and to his utter relief they understood his desperate wish and joined him in song.

'Oh, the seas they know my secret
And the tides and winds they keep
Hidden from the Wanderers far above
A place that's wild and deep.'

A wind swept over the boat, sending Fern-Rae reeling backwards. The sea-kids fell hushed in amazement. Raife himself almost stopped singing, he was so surprised it had worked—the winds had actually stopped the Light Fin in her tracks. But his glory was short lived, for now the violet-haired girl rose with a serpent-like intent and began singing herself. A song Minnow knew, about a mother lost at sea, a child left behind. Its words seemed to claw at Minnow's very soul and she pushed her way to standing.

'Hush sweet child, my little love
Your mother sails out far
Through wild storms
And merciless waves
Guided by a star.'

'One day she will return again
And tell you all she's seen,
One day she'll hold your hand again
Till then, you can but dream.

'Hush sweet child, my little love
Your mother sails out far
Past black rocks
Whirlpools deep
Guided by a star.'

At once the wind obeyed Fern-Rae and began howling fiercely as it swept across the deck.

The wind stung Raife's eyes and Minnow's plaits broke loose and whipped violently around her face. The bird-boys seemed to be on Raife's side now, opening their great wings and shielding him from the terrible winds. Raife and the bird-boys fought Fern-Rae's song by singing the lullaby once more. Minnow darted towards them and sang with everything she had.

'for the call of the sea starts when you're young
And never stops chanting your name
Yes, the call of the sea starts when you're young
And never will you be the same.'

Her voice came out like the light that shines from a full winter moon.

The world fell silent.

There was a crackling of stars and seawater. The tide all at once became very rough, tossing the boat about like flotsam. Lightning carved the night into pieces and many of the sea-kids, frightened, dived overboard. The bird-boys, Fairlith, Fern-Rae, and a boy with stingray fins took refuge behind a sail, their wary faces all peering at Minnow.

'You've woken the High Winds,' Fern-Rae called over the tempest, her face no longer suspicious but astounded. A wave of white foam washed over the deck knocking Fairlith to the floor. She laughed, but her eyes had grown wild with fright.

The storm raged and Minnow's heart beat fast. She stopped singing but the winds didn't halt. In fact, they seemed to grow stronger. 'Get in the galley!' yelled Minnow as the whole of the sky seemed to swoop towards the boat, thunder tearing the skies apart.

The unruly crowd ducked inside and Minnow

bolted the door behind them. 'What's going on?' she asked, a confused fear lodging itself in her heart. The sea-kids huddled under the table, staring at her half in bewilderment, half in adoration.

'You did this. You need to make it stop,' said Fern-Rae, trying to mask her panic.

Minnow shot her a dark look. 'Why should I trust you? You sent orcas after me while you tried to kidnap my best friend. And steal my sea-soul!'

Fern-Rae nodded gravely. 'There hasn't been a sea-soul like *The Seafarer* in the Vintertide for many years. We wanted it.'

Fairlith, blushing, began to sob. We just wanted to distract you long enough to get on your boat. It's lucky for you that you're so fast.'

The wind howled like a gale of demons and lightning struck the mast. Minnow cursed under her breath. 'Well how do I make it stop?'

The boy with stingray fins, called Sting, stepped forward. 'I think the High Winds want to speak to you.'

Minnow frowned. 'The High Winds?' And as she spoke, the door to the galley rattled, as though being shaken by a human hand.

'The storm is trying to get in. Trying to find you.'

Minnow sighed and rubbed her jaw. She was so tired. Her mouth was throbbing from the missing tooth and she was absolutely starving. The last thing she wanted to do was step into a hurricane. The wind screeched louder.

'I'll come with you,' said Raife, who quite honestly was sick to death of being left alone to worry, while Minnow fought killer whales and faced down sharks. But she shook her head with a steeliness that couldn't be argued with.

'Stay with my ship,' she said, the gap in her teeth making her look fierce.

Raife nodded. 'Your sea-soul,' he murmured quietly as Minnow opened the door.

Raife saw a glimpse of a tall man standing on deck, weathered by the sun and older than the tides. He was there, yet he was drifting. Beside him glittered a woman who seemed to be crafted from stardust. It was the same ghostly face he had seen at the window of the lighthouse Lumière all that time ago. Like the man, she was very real, yet also seemed to be floating.

Minnow took a step out into the storm and the door banged shut in Raife's face.

Minnow faced the spectral figures, and felt the world stop around her. Their voices were an echo of high mountain tops and rolling cliffs.

You should not have sung like that.

'Why?'

As the woman drew nearer, a howling bitterness

tore down on Minnow. And even though it was awful, it felt wonderful too, like the taste of thunder. And as this tempest blew, a name began forming in Minnow's mind. A name her mama had told her, not just a bedtime story, but as though it was absolutely real.

'You're the Mistral,' Minnow said.

The woman seemed to like that and Minnow got the sense that she was being curtsied or bowed to by someone in a gown of lightning.

Minnow remembered her mother's words: 'Never upset the Mistral. For she is the bringer of storms which send men to their death.'

There are few who can call us with song. The last was your mother.

'You know my mother?' Minnow forced the words out around the lump that was forming in her throat. The weathered man interrupted her in a dash of golden sand. He was warmth and moonrise and campfire secrets. The Zephyr, Minnow realized, recalling stories of a spirited spring wind, rolling along the coast causing mischief.

We have always known Mercy. When she departed the Deep we followed her to the Far Above, as only the High Winds can. We have watched over you all your life, Minnow.

150

There was such a laid-back quality to him, Minnow could easily imagine him as an old surfer on the Californian coast. He was timeless, yet he was also very young.

And now we are here to warn you.

Surely she couldn't be in any more danger! Minnow wasn't sure she could take much more. The Mistral had become a little flock of white starlings, that swooped and dived around her head, pulling gently at her hair, so her plaits unravelled into a halo of afro curls, and she relaxed.

By calling us with your song, you have shown yourself to the Wild Deep. You possess a rare quality that only Gatekeepers are born with, and because the Gate is without a Keeper, the Wild Deep will want you to stay. To see if the Gate will choose you.

'But I can't stay in the Wild Deep. I need to cross it and rescue Mama.'

We understand. We will carry you across Darkentide. The storm will be your protection.

Minnow found herself smiling with the tiredness that comes from long adventures. She was so grateful to the High Winds. So happy to have the storm as a guide as far as Somertide, and excited by the thought that she might finally come face to face with a real mermaid. Somertide would be the last tide before they reached the Caribbean Sea. Her body was exhausted, but she forced her tired eyes to stay open.

We must not waste time. The dark sea is guarded by a powerful creature called Candlelight, and if he knows of your power he will not let you leave. We will need the strength of song from many voices so that we may help you on this next stage of your journey. Rest now and we will sail at Moontide.

Minnow paled as she realized she would have to ask the sea-kids' help.

Again the Zephyr ran his fingers through Minnow's hair and she smiled. It used to happen all the time when she was little, before she had plaits, a warm summer breeze would tease her curls into knots. 'It was you,' Minnow said fondly, shaking her hair free.

It has always been me.

The High Winds drifted into the air, leaving a small pile of golden sand whirling about her ankles.

Gather your band and get some rest. We leave at Moontide.

Then the winds were gone. The storm quieted and the rain slowed to a gentle rhythm on the decks. Minnow opened the door to the galley and went inside. She did not see the two age-old figures cut from ice and sand swirl at the helm of the boat.

Do you think we should have told her about the Gate?
No. It is better she doesn't know; that was Mercy's wish.

Chapter fourteen

NO MORE SILVER

The galley was in darkness, but for a scattering of starlight which glinted through the porthole. Slowly Minnow bolted shut the door, her fingers still icy from the Mistral's nipping kiss, and peeked under the table. A cheerful sight greeted her. The bird-boys, whose names were Pierre and Pablo, had draped their wings over the others to make a blanket of feathers. From beneath them lay sleepy Fairlith, keen-eyed Fern-Rae, Sting, and a rather windswept Raife.

They gazed warily at Minnow. Her snowflake-sand-glittered hair stood up around her like a crown, and though her eyes were tired, she carried herself like a warrior. 'The High Winds are going help me cross Darkentide, but I need your help.' Minnow smiled hopefully. 'We have to sing together.'

Raife gave a firm nod, but it was not just Raife

Minnow needed to convince.

Minnow pushed her hair back from her face and lit one of the lanterns. Then, opening her mum's emergency tub of biscuits, she knelt down beside the others, a dark-feathered wing welcoming her into the blanket. 'I grew up in the Far Above,' Minnow said softly, knowing that the only story worth its salt right now was the truth. For weren't all fairy tales glimmers of the truth anyway? 'I am a shark-tooth and I am of the Wild Deep, but I am a girl too, from the Far Above. I knew the song to open the Gate. And I knew how to sing to the winds, so we took our chances and here we are. We're crossing the Deep to the Somertide gate. It is a matter of life and death.'

Her words were met with a trembling silence. In the soft glow of the lantern, Fairlith leaned forward and seized Minnow's hands. 'Do you mean . . . ' She caught her breath, her eyes shiny with tears.

'Do you mean that you opened the Gate?' asked Fern-Rae, finishing her cousin's sentence. The air in the room felt very thick and Minnow nodded cautiously.

'You have broken the spell,' breathed Sting, staring at Minnow as if she were magical. 'Candlelight cast the spell and now you have broken it.'

'What spell?' Minnow asked, trying not to sound alarmed.

Outside a wave broke over the deck and the children snuggled further under the blanket of feathers, a flutter of excitement passing between them: a story was about to be told. Raife, who understood the ritual of shared tales out at sea, put the kettle on, fetched a loaf of sourdough, and opened a tin of golden syrup.

'Long, long ago,' began one of the bird-boys, Pablo.

'Not that long,' smirked Fern-Rae. 'I was three when it happened.'

'Fine. Thirteen years ago then,' said the second bird-boy, Pierre, 'the Gatekeeper of the Wild Deep abandoned her duty: she is the one we call the Betrayer.'

Minnow visibly stiffened and Raife almost choked on his sourdough. But Sting picked up the story and kept going. 'The Betrayer vanished into the Far Above before her duty was done. Life went on and everyone assumed the Gate would choose another Keeper.'

'But that's not what happened,' chirruped Fairlith, giddy with glee that her turn had come. 'And then one day a Greenbeard brought a Wanderer girl through the Vintertide gate.'

Minnow and Raife were listening intently.

'The Greenbeard claimed to be in love, wanted to marry his Wanderer,' Fairlith went on, turning to Fern-Rae.

'The Merfins were aghast,' sighed the purple-haired Light Fin. 'Wanderers had always been their greatest enemy, and with no Gatekeeper who knows how many more of her people this Wanderer might have brought in?'

Sting nodded gravely. 'That's when the terrible fight between the tides took place. The Greenbeard died trying to protect his love, and the Wanderer girl escaped with the old shark and was returned back to the Far Above.'

'Wow!' breathed Raife, imagining the glory of swimming with the shark.

'Candlelight put a spell upon the Gate with Old Sea Magic, so it would only open for the next Keeper . . . ' Here Sting faltered, gazing oddly at Minnow again. 'Only the next Keeper never came. The Gate did not choose another.'

'I see,' said Minnow calmly, though her heart was hammering in her chest, matching the swift thrum of the rain against the porthole.

'Who is Candlelight?' asked Raife.

'A peacekeeper of sorts,' piped up Pablo.

'But not one you want to cross,' twittered Pierre.

Fern-Rae twisted a lock of violet hair through her long fingers. 'Since the Gate has been closed, the Wild Deep has become divided.'

An edge of bitterness crept into her voice. 'The Merfins believe the Betrayer was innocent and meant no harm by leaving us, but some other folk of the Deep blame the Betrayer for abandoning us. The Merfins dwell in Somertide, while the Folk dwell in Vintertide. Darkentide is Candlelight's boundary which no one crosses, unless, of course, they have the cover of a storm.'

Minnow took a deep gulp of air. Her eyes flickered to Raife and he gave her the slightest green-eyed wink. *Yes*. Then words were spilling from Minnow's lips like a waterfall of secrets. 'The Betrayer didn't abandon you. The Merfins are right—and wrong—she was protecting the Wild Deep from Wanderers. But mostly she was protecting me, her daughter.'

A melody of gasps swept around the galley. 'The Betrayer has a daughter . . . '

'Her name is not the Betrayer. She is called Mercy and is my mama,' Minnow said fiercely.

Fern-Rae startled everyone by giving a wild scream. 'Do you know the rules about Gatekeepers?'

'They're not supposed to have kids? Yeah, we got that,' said Raife defensively. But Fern-Rae spoke over him. 'Do you know why?' Neither Minnow nor Raife did.

'It's a rule as ancient as the ocean itself,' Fern-Rae said. 'Gatekeepers can't have children because the responsibility of the Gate would pass to the child.' Minnow took a long breath; she was beginning to feel dizzy. Raife handed her a glass of water and Fairlith slipped her little cool hand into Minnow's. Sting squatted down beside her, making a fan from his fins which crackled a deep electric blue.

'No one has been able to open the Gate for thirteen years, apart from you,' he said in a tone of deep gratitude.

'You're either a breaker of spells or you're the next Gatekeeper.'

Minnow felt numb. So many thoughts were tumbling through her mind. The beast. *Her shark*. He had not been hunting her but calling to her, trying to find her through dark water and deep dreams, to draw her to the Gate.

Her song, *her lullaby*. The only thing that could ever soothe her from her terrors. Was it luck that Mercy had sung that song, over and over, like an incantation? Or had she also known the Gate was calling to her daughter?

Mercy. Mercy. Her beautiful fearsome mama. Why had she lied to her?

Minnow began pacing the galley, anger flaring in every part of her. Making her skin glow golden. She crashed into things and kicked stuff over with abandon. 'Why didn't she tell me about any of this? Why didn't she show me the Wild Deep?!' she hissed, slamming a fist into the navigation table. The starfish paperweight shot into the air. Sting caught it, moments before it hit the floor.

Then Minnow was marching across the deck, the others nervously watching her from the door. Rain beat down on Minnow like a sky full of daggers and she dropped to her knees hiding her face in the huge, ragged sail. 'Why did she only tell me stupid fairy tales . . . ?'

A shadow fell across Minnow. A boy stood beside her in

the unrelenting rain. A boy with eyes the same unsettled green as the sea. He held open the fairy tale book, his finger pointing firmly to a passage of writing. Raife crouched down and shouted over the thunderous rain.

'Sometimes when a terrible storm threatened the Wild Deep, the Gatekeeper had to give something of themselves to keep the Deep safe: a lock of their hair; a bone; three drops of blood. And in one case, a life.

'She was protecting you. Like your grandma said.'

Minnow sat very still and Raife sat beside her. And though neither of them saw it, two spectral figures hovered nearby, as old and graceful as the sands of time. Both of them bowing inwards, bending the black sail around the two of them so it seemed they were in their own little tent.

'I don't know what it means,' said Minnow between gasps, 'to be the Gatekeeper.'

Raife shrugged. 'I think you're the same as before only you can do more cool stuff. Sing your way into an enchanted ocean, summon the wind gods or whatever they're called—you know, those old guys.'

Minnow spluttered into laughter. 'The High Winds!'

'Yeah, yeah—them.'

She stared at Raife in surprise. He was right. She was quite literally a girl of two worlds: one of water and one of air. Maybe she was the Keeper who guarded both worlds from each other?

She leaned out of the sopping wet sail and beckoned the others to join them. 'Gatekeeper or no, I have to save my mama.'

'That's not your biggest problem,' Sting said. 'If the folk of the Deep find out you're the Keeper they'll never let you leave.'

A cold fear settled upon Minnow's skin.

'Then we'll just have to keep it a secret,' said Fairlith, slipping her hand into Minnow's. Minnow gazed at the wild group clustering around her. The very same who had not so long ago tried to fight her and take her ship. Her sea-soul. *Could she trust them?* She stared at their fierce faces and murderous grins, and her heart said *yes*.

'We will sing with you and see you through to Somertide,' said Sting. 'But we have a long journey ahead and we should rest first.'

They all grouped together in the galley, the blanket of wings surrounding them like the warm embrace of a dove. Though they didn't sleep, they closed their eyes and ceased to talk, lulled by the sea and the star-crossed winds.

Much later Minnow stirred, her mind misty with a half dream about her mother. At once her hands flew to her jaw. Her teeth were killing her. The pain had begun as low ache out in the rain, but now her whole jaw was pulsing with bright bursts of agony. She slipped out from beneath the wings and stumbled to the long mirror at the back of the galley, peering at her shadowy reflection. Kind brown eyes. Wind-whipped hair. Blossom-pale gills and a mouth twinkling with silver. The loose tooth was long gone. Her gum around her three remaining silver teeth was paining her the most. She tugged gently at each tooth. With a rush of blood they came free in her hands, the pain abating and a sharpness filling her mouth. Minnow darted to the sink, spitting blood and trying not to be sick. She let cool water run over her face. Then ever so carefully she cleaned the three silver teeth and placed them delicately inside Mercy's locket.

As she ran her tongue over the gaps in her mouth she felt the tiniest point protruding from each gum. Her adult teeth were coming through. *I really am the girl with shark's teeth*, she thought with a gentle astonishment. *But I'm also the Gatekeeper*. A whisper of excitement stirred through her thoughts. She tiptoed over to where Raife had left the *Tales of the Sea* and began leafing through its damp pages, searching out stories of Gatekeepers. It didn't matter that she couldn't read much Old Norse; she used the illustrations to remind her of the stories she knew off by heart. And again Minnow felt a brightness in her soul, like a newly-awakened star. For it seemed that the Gatekeeper is capable of many more things than just keeping an eye on the Gate.

The rain pattered into silence, moonlight bright as day reflected off the sea, and there came three sharp knocks on the door. Minnow roused her sleepy crew. Moontide had risen and the High Winds had arrived.

Chapter fifteen

DARKENTIDE

Something moved through the Wild Deep. A sea-soul carved in the image of a pirate's dream. It came on a wave of dark water, carried on a storm. Up it rose, this ship of shadows roaring on a tide that would not be changed. It was bold and brave and it was racing with the wind.

The folk of Vintertide, still sailing on in their regatta, noticed the unfamiliar ship up ahead and they sailed towards it. A sea-soul wild with sea-kids and a gleaming shark-tooth girl at the wheel.

At the edge of the regatta, a group of Greenbeards who were drunk on laughter and lemon-ale pulled down a line made of bunting and fashioned a wonky lasso. Sage, the tallest one of the three who had the thickest, twisted beard gave a raucous chuckle and threw the lasso with a fast, unfaltering precision. But nobody onboard *The Seafarer* noticed that their mast was suddenly decorated with a bright loop of flags. Or that a small boat crafted from a Skoda was being crudely towed behind them.

In the centre of the deck Minnow had her eyes closed. She felt the sway of the wind, the force of the sea, the tilt of her ship. She clung to the wheel and sang with everything she had. Tunes that came to her on a whim and a dream. Ballads torn from fairy tales. Lullabies for oceans lost. Songs for sorrowful souls. All around her the crew of sea-kids echoed her voice with eerie folkloric harmonies. It was like listening to the voice of the rain. It was a race to Somertide; a race against Candlelight; and a race for her mama.

As the songs grew louder Minnow felt the wave beneath them rise. She laughed, her voice breaking into a dazzle of giggled notes. The winds screamed harder and the hull of the boat rose out of the water. Minnow opened her eyes in astonishment, but somehow kept singing. Raife gripped the edge of the crow's nest, his mouth falling open in wonder. The bird-boys' wings dropped still upon the deck, and the sea-kids gasped. For the boat was no longer riding the wave. *The Seafarer* was flying.

Over the edge of Vintertide they soared, and across the waters of Darkentide. None of the sea-kids had ventured this far across the Wild Deep before. The bird-boys had seen it from the sky, but not up close. There was a collective sigh of wonderment as they hung over the side of the boat. For the dark sea was an ocean dreamed by magic. The waves were darkest indigo and seemed endlessly deep, and through them dived and swooped a thousand resplendent beings who lit the sea like fire.

'It's like a lake of living lanterns,' said Fairlith, laughing.

The glittering folk of Darkentide flocked towards *The Seafarer*, leaping from the sea like flying fish, reaching up with long webbed fingers and attaching themselves to the wood.

'What do they want?' Minnow whispered to Fern-Rae, a fluttering sense of unease taking hold. But the purple-haired girl only shook her head anxiously, and handed Minnow back the metal hook.

'These are Candlelight's people. They are trying to stop us passing.'

Below them in the belly of the black ship came a keening chime. *The clock*, thought Minnow, locking eyes with Raife. What was it warning them of this time?

'We're almost across, we're so close. But we shouldn't have crossed Darkentide without Candlelight's permission,' said Sting quietly.

Minnow, Raife, and the sea-kids glanced at each other with the same fierce intention. *Stay together. Fight as one.* They grouped closer. Minnow stood taller. She opened her mouth to command her crew, but at that moment the whole ship suddenly went down, wrenched from the breath of the winds by a thousand scaly hands, the night waves closing right over the crew's heads.

Minnow's first thought was Raife. *He won't be able to breathe if they take him too deep*. She dived towards him, slicing through the nylon line with the metal hook, then dragged him towards the bird-boys. 'Take him up. Find air!' Raife was quite amazed to hear Minnow speak underwater, and then he was clasped in the soft embrace of wet feathers, and the youngest part of his heart was smiling.

As they broke the surface and he watched the pale shape of *The Seafarer* sink down into Darkentide, Raife didn't feel *too* worried. At least not about Minnow. He was, however, slightly more concerned about his own predicament. Flying with the bird-boys was rather risky and still every so often he would find himself plunging crazily downwards, only to be hauled savagely back up again. The effect was like a rollercoaster that really might kill you. Then he saw a small vessel bobbing along behind *The Seafarer* and pointed towards it with a mild exasperation.

The bird-boys pecked, nodded, and crashed right through the Scottish flag sail, skidding to a burning halt upon the Skoda-float's small square deck. A roar went up from the Greenbeards and Raife wasn't sure if they were about to enter into a fight or be welcomed to a party.

He staggered to his feet and cautiously approached

them. They looked mostly human, all with ivy-dark hair and skin that sparkled the pale green of algae. Up close their beards really were quite marvellous. Twisted and gnarled like aged branches, they were the green of moss and spring mornings, and Raife felt sure that if ever he could grow such a beard it would warm his heart to contentment. There was a roughness to the men's manner which caused the bird-boys to ruffle their feathers. Yet Raife had spent his whole life around sea-loving folk and guessed the code and etiquette would be the same even across these worlds. The men looked like mariners of old.

'Cut the bunting,' he shouted, giving a salute and pointing to the string of bunting trailing into the sea, still attached to the sunken *Seafarer*.

The men cried 'Aye aye!' and to the bird-boys' amazement did exactly what Raife said. And not a moment too soon.

The Seafarer was now deep underwater, being dragged towards Candlelight's lagoon. Strange sea creatures began looping over the top of it in a ring of underwater electricity. The effect was mesmerizing. Minnow found herself being drawn towards the display like a sea-wolf is to moonlight. But her shoal closed in around her.

'Don't look at their scales,' warned Sting, sweeping

his great fins around Minnow to break her stare. 'We'll have to leave the sea-soul. Swim for the surface.'

A jolt of anger flared in Minnow. She couldn't abandon her ship. Minnow shook her head, then a shadow lingered at the edge of her vision. A terrible feeling slithered down her spine. She snapped her head around. Nothing. The others stared at her—they had sensed it too. A worried pulse ebbed through the water. *Swim away*, Minnow urged, trying not to think about what she was doing: deserting her home. *It's the only way.* If Candlelight had the ship they at least had a chance of escaping. She took the hook and cut the nylon line, setting the ship free. But the shadow loomed again. This time Minnow just caught the shape of it. A long, scaled beast with frilled teeth and a barbed tail. Not just one of them but several. *What are they?* Her thoughts were answered by Fern-Rae: *Draco-Mere. A sea dragon.* Minnow's heart fluttered as the dragon coiled nearer. She thought of the Greenland shark and how he had been tamed when she glowed. She gathered her courage and shone and dazzled with everything she had.

The light sent ripples through the sea, pushing the creatures back.

A cool hand touched hers and there was Fairlith, fins shimmering like wings, twirling in support, giving Minnow strength. Something leered from the shadows and Minnow saw the snake-like mouth, and bright red eyes, lunging at the Light Fin.

'NO!' Fear rushed in, her adrenalin spiked, and Minnow flew at the creature, darting between Fairlith and the open mouth of the sea beast, her own teeth bared and her skin flaring like lightning.

Sting and Fern-Rae rounded in horror, managing to grab Fairlith by the ankles and drag her towards the surface.

Minnow's spine unfurled, legs locked together and she flew through the sea, defiance and rage pressed together in her bones. She thought of her mama and she brandished the hook. The dragons formed an endless ring, as if they were one single deadly snake, and together they swooped.

And then, just when Minnow thought all was lost, a sudden harmony filled the water, powerful and startling and sweet, and Minnow was frozen. The sea dragons retreated into the murky depths. A sense of wonderment swept over Minnow. *There have always been Mer.* Minnow lowered the hook.

They have swum through the seas of every time and culture, and have as many names as the night: Merrow, Ondine, Selkie, Siren. But those who dwell in the Wild Deep have always been known as Merfins.

Minnow found that for the first time since entering the *Wild Deep* she was speechless.

Chapter Sixteen

MERFINS

Minnow could not take her eyes from the mermaid. She was majesty made from sealight. Her skin was the night dark of childhood dreams. Her eyes were speckles of moonlight. Her indigo hair was woven into salt-bound locks wrapped around a spiked conch shell. But the thing that stopped Minnow's heart was her tail. Brighter than the first flame of the first fire ever struck. It glittered with scales of clementine orange, layered with gold and scarlet, with fins of fearsome ruby.

What do you think of when you imagine a mermaid?

It was Mercy's voice that spoke up from her memories. Minnow had been young, maybe not even four. They'd been lying on the deck of the boat, Mercy's hook sparkling between them.

A maiden pale as a moonbeam, with the silvered tail of a fish.

Little Minnow nodded.

Hair of gold or crimson, or even candyfloss pink.

Little Minnow leapt up and ran to fetch the pink wig from the dressing-up box, determined to be this creature of legend.

Eyes of ocean blue or brightest aquamarine.

Little Minnow laughed, but Mercy had caught her daughter's tiny wrist, tipped Minnow's chin up with the curve of her hook. 'No,' she had smiled firmly. 'Those are the storybook mermaids. Real mermaids are more magical. The real mermaids look like you.'

The mermaid smiled and Minnow felt a deep sense of trust. With a gesture that seemed to hold the authority of oceans, the mermaid opened her strong arms and Minnow raced into them. And there she stayed for some moments bathed in the mermaid's ethereal glow.

'Come, daughter of Mercy,' said the mermaid playfully, 'we'd better rescue your friends.'

Minnow would have done anything she asked, swum anywhere in the world just to be near her, fought any battle, faced any danger. So many feelings collided inside her mind. A sharp aching regret that she had grown up so far from this world. And the bitter understanding of why her mother had lied to try and protect her. And strangest of all, a little beat of empathy for the Sea Hunters. For maybe if Minnow had been a regular child—whatever that was—and she had been swept out to sea and saved by a Merfin, wouldn't she have wanted to share that wonder with the world? With a quick sadness, she realized that was the very thing the Merfins needed protecting from. *They are too astonishing for our world.* The mermaid beat the sea with her tail and all Minnow's thoughts were swallowed by awe, for there was a quickening of the surf and the water became streaked with colour.

Minnow held her breath as mermen with skin that glistened dark as thunder, or bronze as lost treasure, dived by her, their speed unmatched by any fish. They wore their dreadlocked hair like a festival of the tides, embellished with small rusted anchors, forked spears, and sharp-edged shells. Merwomen who gleamed honeyed gold, sun-kissed brown like Minnow, or midnight violet swept past her, their tails a dream of paradise crafted by the waves. Their locks, every colour of the ocean, were threaded with lilies and crowns of coral. Minnow spun amongst them quite bedazzled. The fire-tailed mermaid pulled a short spear from her hair and pointed swiftly to the surface, and with a skittering of fins they broke the surf together.

Raife, the bird-boys, and the Greenbeards were squashed uncomfortably into the Skoda-float all sipping lemon-ale.

Even in the dark Raife saw the shimmer of something extraordinary just ahead. At once he understood what the two boys in the story had felt in Barbados all those years ago, for gazing at the Merfins was like looking directly into the face of a myth. A myth more beautiful than he could ever have imagined. And swimming with them was Minnow!

Together Minnow and the shoal of Merfins began to push the small sea-soul over the dark waves as Raife and the Greenbeards looked on in wonder.

As they bumped along, the tallest Greenbeard, Sage, spoke quietly with Raife. 'You're not from the Wild Deep, are you?'

Raife shook his head, guiltily. The costume hadn't fooled them. The lemon-ale had made his head a little fuzzy and he felt too tired to lie.

'So how did you get in? The golden girl?' Sage asked.

'I'm good with sharks,' said Raife, a little boastfully, 'so I helped her through the Gate, and stuff.'

Sage chuckled and eyed Raife fondly. 'She helped *you* through the Gate my Wanderer friend. But who altered you?'

Raife paused. 'Altered me?'

Sage nodded rather sagely. 'You know, changed you. So you could exist here without drowning. I don't see a tail or scales or fins.'

Raife looked dumbfounded. Was he supposed to have

a tail? 'I, um . . .'

Sage's green eyes narrowed, and he leaned in very close. 'Old Sea Magic,' he whispered in a voice like smoke. 'Any Wanderer who enters the Deep, will be altered forever by the Gatekeeper. That's the only way you'd survive.'

Raife gave a flick of blond hair. 'Well, I've been kind of busy trying to cross the Wild Deep, so maybe I've not noticed the change yet.'

Sage gave a mighty laugh and ruffled Raife's hair. 'Oh, you'd have noticed the change, my boy.'

He twisted his beard in thought. 'Seeing as we've no Gatekeeper, someone who knew Old Sea Magic should have altered you . . . yet here you are alive and well in the Deep.'

Raife grinned uncertainly. Sage dropped his voice to the softness of a morning wave. 'That can only mean one thing my boy.'

Raife literally had no idea what that might be.

'You've got the Wild Deep running through your veins.'

Raife nodded. 'Yeah, yeah,' and was about to ask more when the conversation was cut short by a rousing yell.

'Somertide ahead!'

They had made it at last—all the way across The Wild Deep to the home of the merfins and the last stop before Barbados-Somertide: Clear sunshine was burning everyone's eyes. Raife's hands flew up to shield his face. He was vaguely aware of splashing as his friends leapt excitedly overboard, into an ocean of crystalline blue. No one was prepared for this sea of eternal summer.

With everyone in the water now, Raife, the Greenbeards and the small crew from *The Seafarer* hugged Minnow. Looking in awe at the Merfins, all of them knew that no matter where their lives might lead them next, this moment amongst the Mer would be the memory they reached for in dreams, or cherished in moments of sorrow. This would be the magic that made every other hope seem possible.

'You opened the Gate at Vintertide, daughter of Mercy,' smiled the fire-tailed mermaid.

'My name's Minnow,' said Minnow softly.

The mermaid bowed her regal head. 'Mine is Amarine,' she said, gesturing around the gloriously warm sea. 'Welcome to Somertide.'

It was dotted with tiny islands more like sand-bergs—each just big enough to hold a single tree. Leaving her sea-crew swimming with the Greenbeards and some of the Merfins, Minnow glided over to a plant like a palm tree, only its bark was the colour of coral and it boasted hot-pink flowers the size of pineapples. As she cooled her face in the welcome shadow, she thought of the desolate loneliness she had felt in Vintertide. The sense of struggle that seemed to cleave to the very air there. She gazed at the richness of Somertide: its gentle waters strewn with floating flowers. Its zigzagging fish radiant as jewels.

Yet the roots of the tree were a little blackened, almost rotten. Amarine swam over seeming to follow her thoughts. 'The tree needs snow, just as Vintertide needs warmth,' she explained, scooping up a handful of yellow grains and pressing them to Minnow's cheek. They were fiery warm. 'The sand holds the heat, the same way ice holds the cold. There used to be a flowing exchange between the tides. But not these last twelve years. Not since the great fight between the tides.'

Minnow winced. 'Because Mama left?'

Amarine leaned in and kissed her brow.

'Nobody in Somertide blames you, little fish. We knew and loved your Mercy just as you do. We understood why she left us—to protect you. Her child. A babe cannot be responsible for the Gate. It would have taken your young life Minnow.'

Minnow fell still as she thought of the terrible choice her mother had to make—giving up the Wild Deep, for her. But Amarine cupped Minnow's chin in her hands. 'Mercy loved you from the moment she felt your little heartbeat. It was the easiest decision she had ever made.'

Minnow stared at Amarine trying to hold in the sob that was rising in her throat. 'But now Mercy is in danger. That's why I'm here. I'm going to rescue her.'

Amarine's face became serious, drawn. 'Danger?'

Minnow was finding it hard to speak, as more and more of the Merfins were turning to gaze at her.

Raife bobbed up beside her. 'Do you know the story of *the girl with the shark's teeth?*' he asked.

Amarine laughed gently and beckoned over another mermaid with hair the blue of cornflowers. 'Zavia knows it better than anyone.'

Zavia was devastatingly beautiful, with rich brown skin and scales the same wild shade as the feathers of a blue macaw, edged in startling silver. She spun onto her back raising her glorious tail into the air. Minnow and Raife both saw it at exactly the same time. A patch of bare skin where three of her scales were missing. Minnow remembered the moonlit pendant around Jah Jah's neck and she gasped.

'You're the mermaid from the story, who got caught in the net,' Minnow breathed.

Zavia bowed her head.

'Do you know where to find the Sea Hunters?' asked Raife, who was trying his best not to be completely and utterly spellbound.

Zavia flashed a mischievous grin. 'Why of course. They came to the Wild Deep all the time as children.'

Minnow cast a quick glance at Raife, but he was equally shocked.

'Mercy smuggled them in. Taught them to hold their

breath for four minutes, to pass through the Gate.'

There were so many things Minnow wanted to ask. But her mind was struggling to find the right words.

'Why?' she managed eventually.

'Because she could. Because even as a child Mercy bent the rules and forced the Gate. Eventually one of the older Gatekeepers used Old Sea Magic to ensure any Wanderers who came through would have to be altered, changed forever, so they could never return to the Far Above. That stopped Mercy bringing the brothers through. But, of course, by then it was too late, the brothers could not give up the Wild Deep.'

Minnow swallowed. She felt a rasping sadness for the two boys, suddenly having all of this taken away from them. Having to give up the Wild Deep forever. But also a spike of tender joy for her mother, a breaker of rules from the beginning.

There came a cry from the edge of Somertide as a wise and powerful merman cut through the sea. His name was Solomon and his whole tail was the iridescent grey of a shark, but marked with black stripes like a tiger. 'Candlelight is here,' he said, speaking directly to Minnow. 'He'll never let you go.'

Minnow felt the urgency in his voice and knew there was no time to think. No time to say goodbye. Not to her friends, nor the Wild Deep.

'Come,' urged Amarine, and Minnow seized Raife's

hand as they were pushed to the seabed by the gentle weight of tails, lithe and strong. The tails lapped over each other, like a series of much larger scales, so beneath them Minnow and Raife were hidden, cocooned in a den of colour.

A shadow fell across the dazzling sea. It lingered then slowly moved on, heading towards the Greenbeards' boat. Minnow hoped desperately that her sea-crew would be OK; it tore at her not to say goodbye to them, and all she could do was trust that the Merfins would protect them too.

The den of tails unravelled, as the Merfins flitted into a diamond-shaped formation. Minnow and Raife were guided to loop their arms over the Merfins' shoulders and hold on tight. Raife was at the front, holding on to a merboy named Astro who wore his hair just like Minnow's, his tail the same stunning turquoise as the sky. In the centre was Solomon, flanked by Zavia, and a mermaid named Tamika with jet skin and a tail the colour of rubies. At the back came Amarine, carrying Minnow. Together they raced towards the Gate between the oceans. The Gate that would lead Minnow to Mercy. *Mama!*

Chapter Seventeen

THE SEA CAVE

Minnow was zooming through the sea. She longed just to swim with the Merfins: understand their low sing-song language, see where they slept, hear their stories. But there was no time, and all the while the enormity of the task ahead loomed at her like a cloud of far off thunder. She looked ahead for Raife and considered how to get through the Gate. Whatever magic had saved his life last time Minnow wasn't sure she could risk relying upon it again. But she needn't have worried. As the Merfins pointed out the Somertide Gate, Minnow saw it was far shallower. A dip down and a hard swim back up, into the Caribbean Sea. Raife would *only* need to hold his breath for four minutes. She hoped.

The pull of the Gate tugged at her bones once more. Raife, who had been unconscious last time they crossed between the worlds, was completely wonderstruck. As

they hurtled towards the Gate, Minnow's lips opened
in song, and all around her the wild sea seemed to still.

'I am soul and song of water
I am fin and bone of star
I was dreamed from waves and moonlight
And my heart has swum so far.

'for the call of the sea starts when you're young
And never stops chanting your name
Yes, the call of the sea starts when you're young
And never will you be the same.

'Oh, the seas they know my secret
And the tides and winds they keep
Hidden from the Wanderers far above
A place that's wild and deep.

'for the call of the sea starts when you're young
And never stops chanting your name
Yes, the call of the sea starts when you're young
And never will you be the same.

'I am cut from myth and marvel
I am scale and tooth and sea
I'll protect our ocean mysteries
If you'll only set me free.

'for the call of the sea starts when you're young
And never stops chanting your name
Yes, the call of the sea starts when you're young
And never will you be the same.

'I will soar towards the starlight
I will calm the surf with song
And if Wanderers dare to follow
Their sweet lives will not last long.

'I am soul and song of water
I am fin and bone of star
I was dreamed from waves and moonlight
And my heart has swum so far.'

As the last note sounded, a tremor ran beneath the ocean floor whipping up sand. The bright sea splintered in front of them; searing crystal light turned everything the colour of stardust. Minnow opened her mouth further and roared into the light. The world crackled like lightning. Then the tide drew apart, curtains opening onto a stage of fierce azure. Minnow, Raife, and the Merfins were swept through into the waters of the Far Above.

A tearing tide snatched them up, swirling them into a whirlpool of sand and dancing plankton. It was like being in a sea of gold. The Merfins grasped for Minnow and Raife's hands. Minnow had no idea which way was up or down, but Zavia managed to guide them, calling, as she swam left and right. Out of the dazzle and sand and sea-dust came a deep answering call. A voice of wave-worn wisdom, with a slow-thudding heartbeat. Something was moving towards them, something effortless and wise, but brutal in its own way. With a furious amount of might Minnow swam to the creature until they came eye to sea-bright eye. The girl with shark's teeth and an enormous leatherback turtle.

His skin was a sheen of hardened ebony, flat plates of black armour where his shell should have been. Seven grooves across his back like the strings of a lute, embedded with thousands of tiny prickles, sharp as Minnow's teeth. Minnow closed her eyes and felt his presence. He was the guardian of the Gate on the other side. He would lead them to safety. She had only to glance at the others and they formed a sleek line behind her, following the ancient beast to the surface.

Minnow gasped and they rose above the waterline, Raife spluttering beside her, but otherwise OK. The sky above them was the blue of purest summer, the sea a lapping loveliness of white waves and soft sparkles. There were no boats. No Wanderers, only the shadow of a rocky cove, and in the distance a smudge of land upon the horizon: Barbados.

Raife began coughing, salt clawing at his throat.

'Can you swim?' A note of doubt crept into Minnow's voice. Raife tried to give a confident nod but his skin had taken on a pale sheen.

Under the water the shadows of the Merfins flitted like a formation of tropical sharks. Zavia surfaced gracefully between them. 'We'll carry you as far as the wavebreak.'

Minnow felt a pressing anxiety tighten her throat. 'It's too dangerous. What if you're seen?'

The mermaid raised a mocking eyebrow. They would just have to be fast.

Minnow bit her lip, crying out in shock as she drew blood. The Merfins broke the surface, smoothly as seals, bright eyes turned to Minnow.

'Your teeth . . . they really are like a shark's,' breathed Raife. Minnow blushed, but the Mer were smiling.

The Merfins towed Minnow and Raife towards the

shore, travelling underwater, arcing up like dolphins, then curling back down out of sight, cutting through rips smooth as glass. But Minnow felt no joy. She was wary of Sea Hunters or other Wanderers. She had to make sure she didn't hand the mermaids to them, the very thing she knew they were searching for, before she had even found Mercy.

Now she was really here in Barbados, having made it across the Wild Deep, everything felt startlingly real. Yet she had no real idea where to look for her mama or how to stop the Sea Hunters if they didn't find Mercy in time. As they travelled along, dipping up and diving low, a plan was whispered between them. A plan of many layers, with twists and turns as sharp as the tide. A plan spun finely as the nylon line used to bait a shark. A plan that made Minnow and Raife feel brightly alive and deeply afraid in equal measure; it was their best chance of finding Mercy before the blue moon rose that evening.

The first step was to find where the Sea Hunters were keeping Mercy. To search for the pink house on the hill where the brothers had grown up, to try to discover where Jah Jah kept his deep-sea treasures, or where he might hide a woman with a hook. So they kissed the Merfins goodbye and swam the last length to the shore. Minnow felt the wet sand underfoot, unstable and not to be trusted. *One step at a time* she told herself, gripping Raife's arm to steady herself, feeling like a mermaid learning to walk. *Step one. Find the Sea Hunters' home. The pink house on the hill.*

The sun-warmed sand burnt their feet, and though her body was exhausted Minnow forced herself to run, to head for the shade of a canopy of palm trees, trunks bent like crescent moons. Behind her Raife tumbled over and began to crawl. Minnow couldn't bear to stop. She launched into the sweetness of the shade, where the ground felt cool as ice cream.

As she sank under the palm tree, trying to catch her breath, Minnow slowly took in her surroundings. It was peaceful, though the air was full of slow buzzing damselflies, and the heady scent of coconut. The sand around Minnow's feet was scattered with begonias and fallen orchids. And a loveliness of birdsong trickled through the air, matched with the steady lap of the waves. The sharp beauty of the place could carve its way into your heart forever, thought Minnow, at once falling in love with it. But she closed her mind to its beckoning call. *Find Mama.*

'Water,' croaked Raife, collapsing beside her. Minnow looked around nervously—maybe she could find a café and ask for some? Then she noticed a man sitting very still by a tree nearby. A little game of dominoes was set up on a folding table in front of him, as if he were waiting for a friend to arrive. The man regarded Minnow and Raife with a comical frown. He took a large green coconut from a collection at his feet, lifted a small axe and sliced the top off the fruit, popping a paper straw into it and wordlessly ambling over and handing it to Minnow. Her throat was screaming out in thirst, but she knelt down and offered the straw to Raife. He took a long thankful sip and seemed to be instantly revived. Minnow tried some and found the same; it was both sweet and salty and wonderfully cool. The man tipped his hat to them. Then seeing their sunburnt faces, especially Raife's, he took a leaf of aloe vera, sliced it open, and gave them some. Raife had never felt more grateful for anything in his life.

Minnow felt a tremble of hope. Amarine had told them to be pleasant, but not to tell anyone where they were going and especially not to mention the pink house on the hill. But this man seemed sincere and helpful. Minnow hoped against hope she was right. Speaking through closed teeth, she asked, 'Do you know the pink house on the hill?' The man pushed his hat further up his head.

'The Starrs' house?'

Minnow hesitated. She didn't know the Sea Hunters' surname, so she took a guess and gave a nod.

'Sure thing,' smiled the man. Minnow waited for him to offer up directions. But the man said nothing more.

Raife dusted off his knees. 'We're hoping to speak to Jah Jah,' he said.

Minnow flinched, but Raife ignored her. 'We're really into treasure hunting. We wanted to speak to him about diving.'

He's such a good liar! thought Minnow.

'You'll want his Sea Cave then, up the road, by the bay, just after Speightstown.' He gestured with his arm, to a path leading off the beach. Minnow stared at Raife, her eyes bright with amazement. *His Sea Cave!* If Mercy was going to be anywhere, surely it would be there.

They hurried on in the direction the man had showed them but the heat was wearying. Once they left the comfort of the shade, the rough ground was gravel-sharp underfoot. Minnow's temper flared at the smallest thing: the way Raife breathed, the noise of a passing moped, the way her hair tangled in the wind, the fact it was all taking so long and the sun was already burning hot. Each time they neared the roadside, people kept trying to sell them things. Raife was furious at being likened to a tourist, but Minnow secretly would have liked to look at all the pretty things. The little stone turtles, and starry headscarves, and coral bracelets. She would have loved to have listened to the music that spilled out of people's yards, or tasted the frying fish, but time was ticking. *Find Mama.*

Just when Minnow thought her heart might grow wings, burst from her chest, and fly away with impatience, she spotted a tumbledown structure in the curve of the bay. 'The Sea Cave!' Her whole body began to tremble. It was not a literal cave, but a wind-beaten shack, nailed together with rust and raw defiance.

'Hide in the seagrass and I'll see if anyone's there,' said Raife.

'Do you remember what she looks like?' asked Minnow.

'Sure thing,' answered Raife. 'Hook, silver teeth, red hair—I won't miss her.'

A pang of fear stung Minnow. She did not want to be alone. She did not want Raife to face the Sea Hunters alone. But she couldn't risk them seeing her. Not yet. She nodded, hugged Raife as hard as she could, then unclipped the hook from her belt and pushed it into his hands. 'Just in case . . . '

Raife did his best not to look anxious. As Minnow wriggled into the long grass, he ambled towards the shack, as calmly as he could manage.

He was inches from the door, when it flew open as if thrown by a hurricane. There stood a man who moved through the world with a sense of wild fury, a mermaid scale glittering at his throat: Jah Jah.

Minnow gasped. Jah Jah was easily one of the most charismatic men Raife had ever encountered, and for a moment he was genuinely lost for words.

'Yes?' Jah Jah barked.

Raife went with his instinct. 'Wow! I finally get to meet you,' he cried, launching into a monologue about how he dreamed of searching out the wrecks around Death Rock Cove. Bringing long-lost gold to the surface. Swimming with reef sharks. Jah Jah eyed him with a smirk of amusement.

'What do you want kid?' His voice was surprisingly gentle.

'I want to be you,' announced Raife, feeling he had to go big with his performance. Jah Jah gave a deep rumbling laugh. 'I want to learn everything you know about diving. The kind of maps you use, the equipment, how you learned to go so deep. And what I'd really love more than anything is to see your Sea Cave.'

Jah Jah chewed the side of his lip and considered the boy standing before him. 'It will cost you,' Jah Jah grinned. 'Let's say, ten dollars.'

Raife did not have any money, but he thought of the fairy tale book and he smiled.

Now, on the shores of Barbados at that very moment, two young brothers were haggling for a boat. They had given up their shoes, they had given away a stolen wheelbarrow, they had even parted with a watch they had won in a game of cards.

'I spent my money on rum—for my mum. I lost my shoes in a bet and my wallet in a fight. But if you let me inside, anything I find when I dive you can keep.'

Jah Jah rolled his eyes, about to shut the door when

he saw the hook still clasped in Raife's hands. He stared at it a long moment. 'I gave a girl a hook like this once,' he murmured, almost to himself.

'Nice gift,' Raife grinned. 'Did she like fishing?'

Jah Jah blinked sadly. 'Not at all. There was a storm and the Gate took a bone from her.'

Raife coughed to try and mask his alarm. Jah Jah snapped out of his daze and nodded decisively. 'OK, you can come for five minutes. But don't touch anything.'

Then Raife was stepping into a cave of marvels beyond his boldest imaginings.

Chapter Eighteen

THE BLUE MOON

The shack was a wreckage of rusted boats, salvaged figureheads, sunken hunks of marble, and artefacts from long-forgotten times, all strewn across the floor and balanced on top of each other. Spilling from within one of the rusted boats was a box full of gold coins, like real pirate treasure. In the middle of the room was a cube-shaped tank, full of bubbling water and seashells. Waiting quietly for a myth perhaps?

Raife looked around and figured there were enough artefacts to make Jah Jah a millionaire. Certainly everything you'd need to open a museum and possibly enough strange and wonderful objects to rewrite the books of history. All that was missing was a mermaid. The room was a testament to the love a person could feel for the sea and all its wild, water-bound stories. Being the son of a woman who raised sunken boats up from the dead, Raife knew a fair bit about shipwrecks and treasure, and he very quickly realized three things about Jah Jah:

1)   Jah Jah had a phenomenal amount of courage. There was no expensive diving gear or up-to-date equipment. Just a series of sketches and old maps pinned lazily to a wall, showing where treasure might lie. Which meant Jah Jah must have made the dives himself and swum back up with his gold.

2)   He was not a boastful man. Jah Jah must have seen incredible things and faced many dangers and he didn't seem to be actually famous. Perhaps he preferred to keep his head down, and leave boasting to those who only dreamed of adventure, rather than lived it.

3)   Jah Jah would never give up on the Wild Deep. None of the fabulous grandeur in the shack meant anything to him, no shipwreck could offer him any glory, without the prize of a mermaid.

Outside in the seagrass Minnow was growing fidgety. The blue, breaking waves looked so wonderful and she was so hot and sticky and half the beach was in her hair. Minnow stood up and brushed herself down, unable to keep still any longer. She could feel the rising panic of being on land too long. *Maybe I could just paddle for a minute to cool down . . .*

She slipped off her waistcoat, shoved it in the sand, and began walking directly towards the sea. Suddenly a jeep came hurtling across the sand and drove right up to the waterline. A guy jumped out with sun-bleached hair and Minnow felt the world go still. *Louis.* Her heart slammed against her chest. What if he had seen her? It was too late to go back to the seagrass. Minnow cast about desperately. The beach was busy with Bajan families heading for an evening swim. Minnow gave an inward smile as she saw a group of girls splashing in the sea. *Girls who look like me.* Amongst them—as long as she didn't smile—Minnow wouldn't stand out. A wave rose over her knees cool as silk, and she dived, sinking below the water, peering at Louis from beneath the rushing surf.

He slung something over his shoulder, something thin and silky. He lifted a small jet ski off the back of the jeep, followed by a lightweight raft and a structure that glittered as if it was made of sunlight. It took Minnow a minute to work out it was a fibreglass cage, big enough to hold a person, or dolphin, or a . . . she cursed underwater. She would not let that happen. She tried to lie still and let the coolness soothe her worried mind, as she watched Louis strap the fibreglass cage to the raft, tie the raft to the jet ski, and push both out over the waves. Then he hopped on and started the engine. Minnow surfaced, keeping her face hidden as much as she could, staring as he vanished towards the horizon, a tiny red streak disappearing into Death Rock Cove. The sea turned cold and the sky seemed to spin. Minnow knew in her bones and her teeth and her heart, that's where they were keeping her mama.

She shot out of the sea, running back up the path and almost crashed into Raife as he sauntered away from the shack.

'Your mum's not there,' he said.

'She's at Death Rock Cove,' Minnow answered urgently.

'There's something else,' said Raife, frowning into the sun. 'Do you know why your mum has a hook?'

Minnow shrugged vaguely. To her the hook did not demand a *why*, it simply was part of Mercy. A glittering curl of silver that cast its light over everything. Once folk laid eyes on the hook they quite forgot themselves and saw only a woman who could set their dreams on fire.

'I've no idea. Why?' Minnow snapped.

Raife peered anxiously at the sand. 'I think the Gate took her bone, and Jah Jah made her a hook.'

Minnow's head began to spin. 'So the Gate really does ask a price from its Keepers.' Raife nodded grimly. 'But why would Jah Jah help my mum?'

They both considered this a moment. 'I guess it's like your grandma said—they were all friends until Mercy became the Gatekeeper . . . Maybe he was trying to win her friendship back?'

Raife thought of the captivating man he had just met, the storminess of him, the way the sea seemed to pound in his heart. And yet a sadness had come over Jah Jah when he spoke of the Gate and the girl with the hook. 'I don't know. Maybe he was helping her.'

This made Minnow feel weak with confusion. 'Well whatever happened then, he's not helping her now. He's holding her prisoner at Death Rock Cove.'

Raife swore and sat down hard in the seagrass. They were both exhausted and it was too far to swim to the cove now—even for a shark-tooth.

'Minnow I think we need to move to *Step two* of the plan, we'll have to steal a boat.'

Minnow tried to force a smile. She had hoped so hard that they'd find her mum on land and save her before the sun set and the blue moon rose. But that was now impossible.

Raife put the hook back in her hands. 'Remember you're the Gatekeeper. You can do anything.'

Minnow stood up straighter. She wished she could believe Raife. She wished she felt anything other than absolute dread. Or terror that whatever this night of blue moonlight might ask of her, the Gate could still take a bone. Or every lock of her hair. Or her life.

'Tell me every story you remember reading in the book about Gatekeepers.'

Raife nodded and as they set off to steal a boat he began to recount all he knew, beginning with the conversation he'd had with Sage the Greenbeard and ending in the stories of the fairy tale book. Minnow listened closely to everything and the soft twinklings of a new idea started to form. Just in case everything else failed. It was a terrible risk—but one she was willing to take.

Night fell across the West Indies, thick and rich and wonderful. Soft waves lapped, crickets called, small frogs answered. It pulsed with energy, echoing secrets and laughter, carrying the scent of the sea and wild flowers. And through the dark, a cool wind murmured. It skipped and scuttled like a child through the long grasses around Speightstown. It turned up the sand and made it dance like a flock of hummingbirds. It tore at the sails of any late-night sailors, jostling the waves so people turned away from the water, safely moored their boats, and went to sip punch at Oistin's Fish Fry, or gather on their porches to gossip.

Inland, the night was heated with a warm desert calm. A breeze that stroked your hair or tickled your neck or made you fall into happy dreams. The trees stirred and whispered, and the night birds chorused. This wind was wise and welcoming and moved across the island with an easy grace, keeping everyone contented and far from the beach. There was just one little sea-carrier, crafted from a canoe and an armchair, with billowing sails cut from a sarong. Minnow and Raife hadn't found a proper boat to steal, so they'd cobbled one together. They found it was strangely perfect.

Moonlight lit the waves, turning them silvery blue, and Death Rock Cove cast its long shadow out at sea. Minnow clung to the makeshift mast and peered ahead. *If this goes wrong* . . . But it would not. It could not go wrong. She would not let it. With shaking hands she bound the boat to a jag of rock on the outer edge of Death Rock Cove, hugged Raife, and as delicately as she could, began to scale the rocky outcrop. She grazed a piece of skin off her foot, drew blood across her elbow, and scratched her hands beyond all reckoning, but the pain hardly touched her. Minnow pushed on in a breathless hush until the rock curled forwards like the tip of a breaking wave and she was able to peer over the top.

Over the peak, Minnow saw a fishing boat with a crystalline bottom, anchored. Reclining in the boat with the ease of someone on holiday was her mama. Minnow almost let out a cry when she saw that her mama's hands and feet were bound—with chains, a metal that her diamond hook would never be able to cut through. Minnow's jaw tightened and her pulse skittered. *Rescue Mama.* Surrounding the boat were the Sea Hunters, each sitting on a jet ski. Jah Jah had joined the others and was now hovering the nearest to Mercy, arms folded, face downcast, hard to read. His hair was bound up in a knot, so the shadow he cast appeared to be wearing a crown. Next to him was Louis: his tanned skin looked paler by starlight. His mood was flighty, as though he couldn't keep still. Minnow flinched when she saw a small harpoon resting across his lap. Behind him was the small raft and the fibreglass cage. *Waiting for a myth.* Minnow swallowed. Slightly removed from the others sat Ely, his skin the same deep colour as the sky, eyes alert, fixed on Mercy.

'Moon'll be up soon,' remarked Louis.

'Are you ready to sing?' Jah Jah's tone was low, steeped in something sorrowful.

Mercy tilted her head to the stars. 'Any requests?' she asked, as though totally unconcerned by her predicament.

Jah Jah chuckled, but it sounded hollow. Despite the heat, Minnow shivered.

'You got two choices. You sing, open the Gate, we get our catch, everyone goes home happy.'

Mercy spat over the side of the boat.

'You don't sing and someone is going to die.'

Mercy stood very suddenly, rising up quick as a snake. On impulse the three men all drew back. Minnow closed her eyes, but no violence came. 'Where does it end, Jah'?' said her mother, hotly. 'Do you think you'll stop at one mermaid?'

'I think I could change the world with one,' he replied.

And even though she hated him, Minnow felt the magnetism of his wish nip at her heart.

Mercy laughed dryly.

'We're ethical people,' reasoned Louis. 'There's so much we don't know about the ocean, so much we could learn from a creature like that.'

Mercy held up her chained wrist and hook. 'Ethical?'

'You almost took my eye out,' said Louis matter-of-factly. 'I had to protect myself.'

Mercy focused on him sharply, her hook catching the light of the moon. 'What's in it for you anyway?'

'I'm a marine conservationist,' he said pompously.

'You mean you want a mermaid for your daughter and you're willing to pay anything to give her what she wants,' Mercy sighed.

Louis gave a baffled shrug. 'Sure. My little girl wants to meet a mermaid. I want to make her wishes come true. And save the ocean.'

Mercy just stared at him as if he were the stupidest man alive.

Minnow bit her lip, trying not to draw blood. It was time for the next step of her plan. *Step three.* Quivering, she turned and waved to Raife in the sea-carrier below. *The Signal.* He stood up, took a long breath, gathered his nerves together, and shouted, 'NO WAY!'

Inside the cove, Jah Jah snapped his head up and

addressed Ely. 'Go see what that's about.'

'I'm not going anywhere,' said Ely calmly. There was a long pause.

Outside Raife silently counted to ten, then shouted again: 'It's a . . . It can't be . . . It's a, it's a MERMAID!'

Mercy visibly paled and Minnow wanted to call down to her—to say, *Mama it's OK, it's part of the plan.* But instead she drew her mouth closed and pulled up her knees so she was ready to dive. Jah Jah threw a furious glance at his brother and started the jet ski. Minnowwatched anxiously as Louis casually swung the harpoon onto his shoulder.

Ely grimaced, his throat tight, but his voice silky soft. 'You can put that down, no one needs to get excited.'

Louis didn't budge. Ely slipped almost soundlessly into the water, swam to the glass-bottom boat and skimmed effortlessly in beside Mercy. Louis couldn't shoot at her without going through Ely. Minnow let out a breath of relief. Then Jah Jah crashed back into the cove on the jet ski, with Raife slung across the front of it, his collar clasped in Jah Jah's hand, and she gasped it back in. She had known this would happen; it was what they'd agreed. Yet to see Raife handled so roughly made her eyes water.

'How did you get here?' Jah Jah barked.

'I followed you in my boat. I just wanted to watch you dive,' Raife spluttered.

Jah Jah muttered a curse. 'Not tonight kid. Take a jet ski, go back ashore.'

'But there's a mermaid out there. Honestly, her tail is sapphire blue and her fins are silver like starlight. Her scales look just like your necklace.' There was a beat of stillness. Then lots of things happened at once.

Jah Jah spun the jet ski around with Raife still on it. 'Show me where!' he cried as they flew out of the cove. Louis followed, dragging the fibreglass cage along with him.

In the boat, Ely took Mercy's face in his hands. 'Just go. They will never give this up.'

Minnow stood up on the precipice of the rock, readying herself to dive. This was her moment to rescue her mama. She raised her arms into a point.

Mercy shook her head, shook away tears. 'That's why it has to be me. Jah Jah will be fighting to get into the Wild Deep forever.'

Minnow paused to take a breath, her knees bent in diver's stance.

The boat rocked as Ely fell to his knees, his face both angry and hopelessly sad. 'Let someone else fight him, Mercy. Go and be with our daughter, I'll hide your tracks, buy you time.'

At the top of the rock Minnow froze. *Our daughter.* She couldn't breathe. The stars were too bright. The moon too fierce. Her foot quivered, she wobbled dangerously, she threw her arms out like wings, caught her balance. But dizziness was clouding her vision. She squatted down, clinging to the rock, trying not to whimper.

A memory came to her fast and bright. She was little, maybe six, helping Mercy clean the draft of the boat. Every time little Minnow surfaced, families clustered closer smiling at her. They were not like her own.

Mercy had scooped her out of the water and told her a story. *A fairy tale.*

'Once a wave and an island fell in love and had a child. A little girl who was part sea and part land. But they could not stay together, as waves need the moon and islands need the sun. So they chose to love each other from afar. The little girl stayed with her mother learning the rhythms of the sea, and the stories of the land, until one day, many years later, she was ready to visit the island.'

Little Minnow had accepted this. Mercy and Miyuki were her entire world. They were her family. Whenever they had spoken of her father over the years it was with a sense of fantasy, as if he wasn't quite real. And yet here he was.

There came a rumble of jet skis as Jah Jah returned, and hot tears fell from Minnow's face. She had missed her chance to dive.

She hardly heard the argument unfolding in the cove, the two brothers shouting at each other as Jah

Jah dragged Mercy out of the cove. Minnow closed her mind to everything but the night, climbed numbly down the rock, and slipped into the sea unseen.

The blue moon rose, the water glinted an eerie turquoise, the tide turned, rolling swiftly back on itself becoming steadily lower, and from outside the cove Louis gave a shout. 'I can see the Gate. It looks awesome.' The jet skis chugged out towing the glass-bottom boat, with Mercy tight-lipped inside it.

Raife, who was now perched on the raft beside Louis, gazed about uneasily. *Where's Minnow?* He tracked back over the plan in his mind and scoured the rocks for Minnow. But she wasn't there. Which meant the dive hadn't worked, and they needed *Step four*.

Beneath the surface of the water Minnow watched as the jet skis towed the boat out. All eyes were fixed on Mercy, who sat defiant and unmoving, Ely beside her, his brown eyes wide with worry.

Louis raised the harpoon. 'Time to sing.'

Mercy made no sound, but stood in a state of fury, her chest facing the harpoon. Ely again moved in front of her, causing Jah Jah to leap up ready to strike his brother.

'Look there's something glowing in the water,' Raife half shrieked, his heart soaring with relief. Everyone lurched forwards. Beneath the tide Minnow kicked and spun and soared faster than a bolt of lightning, her skin a dazzle of sealight. From above there was no way to tell what she was: fish, or girl, or myth.

'That's the mermaid!' shouted Louis.

Minnow raced away from the boat; at a safe distance she locked her ankles together, arced her back and shot out of the sea in a dolphin dive, letting a note of song burst from her lips. Raife gasped. *She really does look like a mermaid.*

In the boat Mercy went white with horror. 'No!' she screamed, then her hook was somehow breaking her chains, and Ely was helping her.

On the jet skis Jah Jah and Louis zoomed after the mermaid.

Minnow dived deeper, in a zigzag pattern, trying to draw the Sea Hunters away from the Gate. But Jah Jah and Louis were quicker, and like Zavia before her all those years ago, Minnow did not see the net until it was too late.

It was thin as gossamer, almost invisible, immune to the bite of sharks' teeth. Minnow felt herself being hauled upwards. The moment they saw her legs, it would all be over. Jah Jah would figure out who she was, or Mercy would give it away. *Mama!* Once the Sea Hunters realized she was the true Gatekeeper Minnow would be forced to sing. She had to rescue her mum and the Wild Deep. That was her duty, the very thing Mercy had tried to save her from, but it was too late. There was only one final step of the plan she could take. It was the last resort and it made Minnow sick with dread to think of it, but somehow she had known it would always come to this. She took a gasp of sea salt and courage. Opened her mouth and sang from the bottom of her soul.

There was deafening crack as the sea split. A rip in the middle of the dark tides, gleaming silver. Jah Jah and Louis both fell back. The Gate was opening. Mercy, now free of her chains, dived from the glass-bottom boat, her eyes on the net. But Jah Jah had already let go, his heart yearning for the Wild Deep.

'Come on!' he yelled, and Louis shook his head, trying to haul Minnow up.

'We've got our mermaid—let's go back home.'

Mercy surfaced beside Louis, striking him so hard it almost knocked him out. The net gave way. Mercy dived for her daughter. There was a single moment of wonder, when Minnow felt Mercy's warm embrace, the softness of her cool skin, the familiar curve of the hook. They were together. Mercy was safe—*almost*. In the deep, dark sea they held each other and the pain in Minnow's heart unfurled. *Mama*. But Jah Jah was swimming for the Gate. Minnow flitted out of Mercy's arms, and they both shot after him, swimming side by side.

Mercy reached him first, appearing in front of him like a sea spirit, forcing him back with her diamond-edged hook. 'You can't go through; it'll kill you.'

Then Ely was beside them trying to wrestle Jah Jah away. Raife leapt off the raft and tried to grab Jah Jah by his ankles.

Louis, still dizzy from his knock, called out, 'Jah Jah, listen mate, it's too deep; we'll never make it through.' But there was no stopping Jah Jah, his desire was greater than all of their strength. He soared down towards the shimmering Gate dragging Ely and Mercy with him. On the surface Minnow and Raife stared at each other in the moonlight. Louis was already heading back to shore, to get help, or return to his family and forget the whole thing ever happened. The two friends held hands. They didn't have long and if the magic really worked who knew what would happen. Minnow would have to give a sacrifice and Raife might never be the same again. Or worse.

'Ready,' grinned Raife. Minnow gripped his hand as though she might never let go of it.

'You're the best friend I've ever had,' she mumured. Raife gave a shy nod.

'Yep, me too,' he mouthed. Then together they dived.

Minnow shut out the world, letting in only the sigh of the ocean. She was the Gatekeeper. It was up to her who crossed between the worlds, and as the ruling went, if a Wanderer did stray into the Wild Deep, it was up to her to let them die—or alter them forever.

She alone could spare their lives and change them,

or let them perish like so many before. *Find what's in your soul.* She had a shark's soul. That was her bloodline. The oldest bloodline, the original Mer. The muses from which legends were born. Songs and folklore and stories of mermaids had woven their way through her childhood. And it was that which rested in her soul. Minnow focused her mind and wished. The Old Sea Magic did the rest.

As they burst through the Gate between oceans there was a darkening in the bright water and Minnow tasted blood. A groan of agony. Then peace.

The Gate whispered shut behind them, a sweeping wave carried them up to the waters of the Wild Deep. Minnow, Raife, and Mercy all broke the surface together. Somertide was bright, and the air had a surreal quality to it. Minnow looked around. Where were the Sea Hunters? Vanished? Dead?

Pain carved into Minnow's jaw and she gave a gasp, almost fainting.

'Your shark's teeth,' murmured Raife, but even as he spoke the four shark teeth that had sprung from Minnow's jaw just yesterday dissolved like mist into the water. Mercy's face was tight with sorrow. She pulled Minnow into her arms: 'Oh my darling, what have you done . . . ?'

Chapter Nineteen

MINNOW'S WISH

Minnow and Mercy clung to each other, pulling Raife into their huddle. Minnow was deeply afraid. *What have I done?* A life force began flickering into being somewhere in the sea below them. Minnow could feel the kick and pull of it. The absurd disbelief, the heartbroken fury, the wonder. They came up from the Deep in a single silver wave. Two beautiful Merfins. Minnow had known somewhere in her heart that this was the consequence of bringing Wanderers into the Deep. But to see them. To know she had done this, brought both a startling sorrow and a quiet sense of amazement.

Jah Jah began thrashing around wildly. His tail was a magnificent, vivid purple with fins of deepest green. 'What's this? What's this???' His voice so sore with regret it was hard to listen to. 'What did you do?' he breathed, staring at Minnow in such a state of anguish she had to turn away.

'You've got your mermaid after all, Jah Jah,' said Mercy, her voice low with warning. But it was Ely who calmed everything down. Ely who pulled his brother into an embrace and stilled his rage. Talking him gently through everything, gazing at his own coral-bright, silver-scaled tail, the way a child first gazes at a butterfly.

Minnow was still tightly clasped in Mercy's arms. *Mama.* There was so much to say, but Minnow's words were lost to relief. She kissed her mum, breathing in salt and gin and lemons, then spun suddenly around to Raife. 'Did anything happen to you? I mean are you altered? Are you OK?'

That had been the biggest risk, that by saving the Sea Hunters' lives, by altering them, Minnow might die, or Raife would be caught in the spell and altered forever too. He gave a little shrug. 'Nope. Same old, same old. I've been through the Gates three times now and I don't feel different.' It was odd. But there was no time to question it. All around them the sea was lighting up with the dart and dive of other fabulous-tailed mermaids. Zavia flew into Mercy's arms and the two women hugged each other as if no wave would ever part them. Then she turned gracefully to Jah Jah, swimming right up to him, brown eyes to brown eyes and as he gazed at her, he finally quietened. For this was the mermaid he had caught by chance all those years ago, in his net and in his heart.

All around them other sea-souls were appearing, carrying folk from Vintertide. And the sea began glimmering with night-magic as creatures from Darkentide arrived. It seemed Sage and the Greenbeards weren't the only ones curious about who Minnow was and why she had crossed the Deep on a storm. Mercy's hook glittered in the sea-light and Minnow felt herself tremble. Would the Wild Deep forgive Mercy for abandoning them? Would they accept Ely and Jah Jah? Would she be forced to stay?

A man who was part fish, part flame stepped out of the water onto a sand-berg. Minnow couldn't tell if he was very old or simply very grand. His skin was the deepest black she had ever seen, his eyes brightest blue, and along his spine and every limb were spiked fins that moved and glowed like fire: Candlelight.

Minnow felt her mama tense beside her. She saw the Mer turn their bright-eyed faces towards Candlelight. She spotted her shoal of sea-kids, in the Greenbeards' sea-soul and noticed how they all fell silent. Fear prickled her skin, but Minnow shook it away. She had faced a shark, summoned the High Winds, and tricked the Sea Hunters; she would not let herself be afraid. Under the water Raife found her hand and she glanced at him gratefully.

'Remember you're the Gatekeeper.'

Minnow gave a small smile, let go of Mercy and Raife and swam forwards into the dancing glow of Candlelight's fins.

'The Wild Deep is a place of magic, a land of myth and dreams. You opened the Gate, so you will stay and be our Keeper until the Gate chooses another.' His voice held an authority that could not be argued with.

Yet another voice cut through it, like a blade of ice. 'No.'

Mercy stood upon the sand-berg, hook glittering dangerously. The folk of the Deep drew back, quite aghast to see her. 'She is twelve. The Gate has already taken her shark's teeth. I will not have it take her life too.' There were shouts and screams of rage and disapproval aimed at Mercy, the Gatekeeper who had betrayed them. Minnow felt the tide begin to turn. She raised her face to the sky and sang.

An ice wind whirled through the Wild Deep, drawing the remaining folk from Vintertide and Darkentide together with all of the Merfins in Somertide. No one ever argued with the Mistral. Soon all in the Wild Deep were assembled.

The Zephyr lifted Minnow up in one arm, and with the other hand he reached into a pocket sewn from sky and emptied out a handful of golden sand. As the sand hit the water it formed the shape of a single silvery palm tree, the centre of its branches curling into a regal chair.

A throne of musk stems, leaves, and sea-mist. Softly Minnow was lowered into the throne. She gazed at the gathered crowd; a little barb of nervousness stung her until she spotted her sea-crew, their smiles urging her on.

'I was a Girl with Shark's Teeth,' she began, a small ache of regret blooming in her heart. 'I am Mercy's daughter, Gatekeeper of the Wild Deep.'

Shocked murmurs rent the air. Some were still furious that Mercy could have broken the rules by having a child. Others were full of empathy. The High Winds silenced them with the screeching threat of a storm.

'I opened the Gate, and altered these Wanderers for their protection and for ours. They will live with the Merfins in Somertide.'

Minnow paused as the folk of the Deep regarded her in amazement. What was the answer? Should she stay and be the Gatekeeper? Would Mercy be welcome too? If they left to go home what would it mean for the Wild Deep?

A voice smooth as summer sea-light spoke up. Ely. 'I will guard the Gate till it chooses another Keeper. Minnow is part Wanderer too, and she must be free to live in both places.'

Everyone turned to glare at this merman. Minnow thought he looked strangely magnificent, the ends of his neatly-woven dreads were already turning aquamarine.

'What could you possibly know about protecting the

Deep?' came a cry of resentment.

Mercy spoke gently over everyone, her voice low like a whisper. 'He has been protecting the Wild Deep his whole life, keeping the Gate a secret but from the other side. He knows the ways of the Wanderers better than anyone.' Here she risked a gentle glance at Jah Jah, whose mood was still as dark as death. 'Ely knows the lengths a man will go to catch a mermaid.'

Jah Jah spat furiously, but Zavia laid a soothing hand on his arm and Minnow thought she saw him soften.

It was Candlelight who made the final decision after hearing everyone speak. He consulted Mercy, listened to the Merfins, to the folk and creatures from both tides. Spoke with the new arrivals Jah Jah and Ely, and finally he spoke alone with Minnow. And he saw just how fearless she was and what a great Gatekeeper she would make. *So like her mother.* But he also knew the risk of keeping Minnow here was too great. There was a year left. A single year until the Gate would chose another as it did every thirteen years. They had made do this long without her, they could manage a little longer. When Candlelight had looked deep into Ely's eyes he saw that this merman could certainly guard the Gate until then. He would not be as powerful as the girl, but strong all the same. So it was agreed by ritual of the tides that

Ely would assume responsibility for the Gate until the Gate chose another. A man who understood the magic of the Merfins. A man who had always been enchanted by the Wild Deep, from the first moment he glimpsed it through the eye of a storm. A man who was related to the Gatekeeper.

It was with great reluctance the Wild Deep accepted that Minnow and Mercy should be free to move between the oceans, the Deep, and the Far Above. It would take a while for Mercy to be forgiven. But the Mer had her corner, and secretly many of the Wild Deep were simply relieved she hadn't abandoned them, so long had they yearned to hear her laugh and to see her smile.

As for the tides, they would no longer be divided. With Ely to protect the Wild Deep until a new Keeper was chosen, there was much to prepare in the coming year, and all three tides would need to work together if they were going to train the next shark-tooths.

Finally Mercy smiled and Candlelight gave a nod to end the gathering. The Zephyr playfully ruffled Minnow's hair and the Mistral became a cloud of diving swallows. Minnow felt herself wilt with relief. Then there was a manic flapping of feathers, and darting of pale fins as the sea-crew rushed over.

Minnow leapt down from her chair and tumbled into their arms. 'Things turned out kind of strangely,' she grinned.

'You rescued your mum just like you said you would,' said Sting kindly.

'Altered the Sea Hunters,' added Fairlith.

'Lost your teeth,' chimed Fern-Rae.

'But no one died,' twittered the bird-boys.

'I couldn't have done any of it without you,' Minnow said softly, suddenly worried she might cry.

'You're so lucky,' grinned Raife. '*You're a girl of two worlds.*'

She had always been. Part black, part white. Part Wanderer, part shark. Part fairy tale, part fact.

There was a gentle splashing, and Minnow turned to see a merman with a coral-bright tail and a welcoming grin. Face to face the likeness was unmistakable. Same smile. Same bright brown eyes. Different teeth. Ely's eyes filled with joyful tears and he reached out and gently touched her cheek. 'Hello, little fish,' he said in that sing-song tone of his.

She smiled, and Ely's hand trembled slightly. 'My name is Elius but most folk call me Ely.'

'My friends call me Minnow,' she replied, feeling the touch of the High Winds ruffling her hair, 'but my true name is Amelie.'

Around her the sea-crew and Raife all blinked in surprise, but the bird-boys squawked in agreement. 'But of course,' they chorused, 'it means defender.'

Slowly, Ely and Minnow moved away to a quieter

sand-berg where they both sat, Minnow's brown legs trailing in the sea next to her father's glorious tail. 'Do you think you'll be OK—being a merman?'

Ely gave a soft smile. There was such a peacefulness to him, that Minnow found herself resting her head upon his shoulder. 'I think I will get used to it. Sure I'll have to watch out for all the plastic bags wrecking the ocean and make sure I can outswim the reef sharks . . . But who else will get to live this dream?' Minnow nodded. 'And if I miss home I can swim ashore by moonlight.'

'But—' began Minnow.

'No one will be looking for a black merman,' Ely beamed. 'I'll be able to stay out of sight.'

'I don't know,' Minnow exclaimed, thinking of the Bajan flag she had seen fluttering around the island. 'The flag is marked with a trident. Perhaps people have always thought there were Merfins in the Caribbean; perhaps you're what they're waiting for.'

Ely quietly chuckled at this, then another striking merman swam over, his mood resigned, his brow creased: Jah Jah. He was still hovering on the edge of fury, but seeing Zavia again after so many years had eased this a little. First, he'd felt regret for the years of his life given to pursuing her. Then anger that he would never be the first man to prove the Caribbean Sea was home to mermaids, then a strange and unexpected flicker of joy.

As Minnow subtly glanced at him, she was struck again by the thunderstorm grace of him, the way the sea seemed to have swept into his heart. The way he moved with a jagged swiftness. The way already his tail had a dangerous majesty. He was almost more shark than her.

'What about all my stuff?' Jah Jah said.

She thought of the shack full of wonders Raife had described. 'Perhaps we'll open a museum, in your name,' she suggested.

Jah Jah looked at her slyly, still angry, but it was lessening. He gave a nod, then ruffled her hair. Minnow found she was beginning to like him.

There was, of course, still the problem of Louis and his mermaid-loving daughter. But when Ely and Jah Jah didn't return they could only hope Louis would assume the two men had drowned and turn his attention to other matters. And if they did happen to run into him in Barbados—well, he was pretty weary of Mercy and would likely keep his distance.

Gazing around Somertide Minnow saw Raife was with the Greenbeards, who were all learning Solomon's songs. Fern-Rae and Sting were sat chatting to some Darkentide folk on a sand-berg. The bird-boys were perched upon the little throne arguing over a mango. Fairlith was playing tag with a group of younger mermaids. Candlelight was bringing Minnow's beloved ship back to the surface.

She swam over to join him, raising the ship and its proud mermaid figurehead into the day. The way it was carved, it looked a lot like Amarine. Minnow sprang lightly onto the deck and let the sails out to dry. *Home.* Everything seemed to still be in place. The galley warm with light of lanterns. The ornate clock that told more than just the time. The starfish paperweight, securing the whaleskin map to the navigation table. The fairy tale book beside it, its page opened to *The Girl with the Shark's Teeth*.

Minnow moved across the deck and stood by the wooden mermaid.

Two figures faced each other in the sun bright sea. One a merman, one a woman with a hook. Minnow silently watched them. She wasn't sure what they said, but she had never seen her mother look at any man like that. Most men Mercy was either trying to kill, or flashing them her bewitching smile, or trying to get something from them. Whatever it was they spoke of, both had a glow of serenity. A gust of wind blew a dark cloud across the sun. Ely leaned over and kissed Mercy, just once. Then he let her go, watching as she swam away, looking more beautiful than ever. And with a bittersweet tug of her heart Minnow realized it was time for her, Mercy, and Raife to leave.

No goodbyes were said. For this was not a goodbye, it was simply a parting of company until the next time. They sailed across the Deep on a roar of songs and windswept cheers. Raife was a little quiet on the journey. He hoped so desperately that he'd get to come back next time—whenever that was. He couldn't imagine having to give this all up.

With a rush and a roar of underwater lullabies Minnow opened the Gate, Mercy beside her, quietly marvelling at just how miraculous her daughter truly was. The way she dived towards her shark, pulling Raife alongside so he could live out yet another dream. The way she swam with the power of the sea in her bones. The way she had found her place in both worlds. Mercy had tried so hard to shield her little babe from danger, but the adventure had found Minnow anyway. There were so many more for them to have together. In the Wild Deep and the Far Above.

As they neared the quaint harbour of Reykjavik a loud, moonstruck howl hit Minnow's heart and she dived overboard, graceful as a gannet, and shot towards the shore. There dashing up and down in front of the colourful storybook houses was Miyuki. Minnow leapt out of the water, scattering droplets of salt like pearls, and flung her arms around the husky's neck. Then Minnow was crying, sobbing into wolf-like fur. How she had missed her best friend.

Raife hopped out and wound the painter into a figure-of-eight knot, and in a single bound Mercy joined him. Then there came the sound of wheels over the gravel. They looked up to see Old Gunnar in a clapped-out, half burnt car. Raife was quite astonished—he had never seen the old fisherman drive before. The door creaked open and Gunnar got out, cap in hand. But there was someone in the passenger seat, someone ghostly pale.

'Grandma!' Minnow screamed, bolting towards her, but she stopped moments before reaching the car. Something was wrong. She could feel it. Slowly she opened the rusted door. Her grandmother, such a fierce force of nature, looked ever so frail. So tired. Her eyes, glassy. And Minnow understood in that moment that there wasn't much time. That the air was hurting her grandmother and despite her battling spirit, she needed the sea.

'You're going, back aren't you?' Minnow cried, tears streaming down her face.

Arielka nodded. 'It's my time.' Minnow sprang into her arms, clinging to the old woman so tightly it seemed she would squeeze the life from her.

Then Mercy and Raife were beside her too.

'That's why you sent my only daughter into the Wild Deep without a guide,' said Mercy, pulling her mother into a gentle embrace.

'I didn't want to disappear on Minnow without her knowing where she came from. Couldn't just leave her alone in Iceland, without any family,' Arielka said with a dry, crackling laugh that sounded as if it burnt her throat.

Minnow glared at her. 'You knew I was running away to the Wild Deep?'

Arielka took her granddaughter's face in her hands and kissed her. 'Grandmothers always know everything; we've done it all before, little Minnow. Life moves in a circle, just like your shark.'

Minnow straightened her spine and clasped her hands together as Arielka climbed awkwardly out of the car and moved to the edge of the harbour. 'You know where to find me, my darling. Swimming in the waves of the Wild Deep.'

Minnow forced a smile. Miyuki licked her hand and leaned her soft body against Minnow's leg. It felt like the most comforting thing in the world.

Arielka looked at her daughter. 'Do you forgive me, daughter of the Deep?'

'There is nothing to forgive, mother. You were right, she needed to know who . . .'

But here Mercy turned away, her face wet with tears. 'She needed to know everything she is.'

Arielka found the strength to open her arms and gather everyone into a hug, kissing each forehead or cheek in turn. Then she glanced up at the low setting sun, seeming to forget they existed, listening to a melody that only she could hear. She stepped out of her shoes and slipped into the sea. There was a pure white flash, like a bolt of lightning under the water, and then she was gone.

They all slept on *The Seafarer* that night, telling stories about wild-hearted Arielka, or singing the songs of the Wild Deep as Miyuki howled along. The little flat in the yellow house was to become Minnow's, so she and Mercy would always have a home on the land, should they need it. And it was where they spent their summers anyhow. From the bedroom Minnow was sure she could glimpse odd flashes of light from the lighthouse Lumière, and once or twice she thought she saw a woman swimming out deep with long grey hair and eyes that shone like stars—but she couldn't be certain.

She gave Raife *The Book of Sea-Myths: Tales of the Sea* as a parting gift. Though she would see him next summer, if not before. And once they got new phones they could speak whenever they liked. It was very odd to even think about having a phone: it felt so strange to clasp something so small to pour all your attention into, when there was an entire, wondrous world happening all around you. But they both supposed they would adjust. Just like they'd have to get used to wearing shoes again. Weird.

Raife hurried home, with the precious book tucked under his arm. When he got in, his mum and Viktor were both mightily amused by his get-up. 'I didn't think you were into fancy dress!' teased Viktor.

Raife just shrugged. 'I guess I am.' His mum ruffled his salty hair. 'Fish camp was good then?' she asked gently.

'Fish camp? Oh! Er . . . Yeah, it was . . . magical,' smiled Raife. He popped into the bathroom to wash his tired face. Examining his chin he saw it was dusted with the lightest stubble. Another weird thing: in the bathroom light it looked green . . . Imagine having a green beard—Raife stopped quite still. In the quietest part of his soul a flame had begun to flicker. He ran upstairs to FaceTime Minnow.

Minnow stood at the helm of her home. Mercy was halfway up the rigging fixing a tear in a sail. Tomorrow they would set sail for Barbados, taking the slow route, bringing Miyuki on their adventure this time. They would find Minnow's cousins, stay for a while with Minnow's aunt in the pink house on the hill, and learn the many bright stories of the island. At night they would cross through the Gate between the oceans and swim with creatures of marvel and myth, one of whom was Minnow's father. And perhaps when the hurricane season had passed they would return to Brighton, to gaze across the harbour and swim out far in the midnight tide. Either way, wherever they ventured, the kiss and tug of the High Winds would be with them.

Mercy leapt down and swung her daughter into a salt-kissed hug. 'Perhaps I should have told you, little fish,' she said in a choked voice.

Minnow nodded. 'Perhaps you should.'

Mercy tipped Minnow's chin to the sky with her hook. 'But then you would have begged me to take you there, to let you see the Wild Deep and to sing to the Gate. The Gate takes whatever it likes and I couldn't risk losing you to it.'

Minnow nodded. It had all been there in stories and songs, this magical world, her own bright history. Minnow just hadn't known it was real. She gazed at the beautiful carved black mermaid on the prow of the ship. 'I used to think she was me,' Minnow smiled, 'but now I know what the Merfins really look like, I know she is one of them.'

Minnow touched the thin nylon thread, still bound round her ankle, exactly the same as Raife's. She was feeling dreamy with tiredness. She flopped into the green hammock and closed her brown eyes, her afro making the perfect cushion, her feet softly moving even in sleep. Somewhere in the deep, dark world below the sea, a shark was singing, softly calling her name, and in her dreams, Minnow's shark heart was glowing.

CERRIE BURNELL

Cerrie Burnell is a writer, actor, and former CBeebies presenter, who has in recent years made a name for herself as one of the most exciting new children's authors on the scene. Her picture book *Snowflakes* was performed at the Oxford Playhouse to great acclaim in 2016 and 'Harper', her young fiction series, has been set to music by the Liverpool Philharmonic Orchestra. *The Girl with the Shark's Teeth* is her stunning debut for middle grade readers.

ACKNOWLEDGEMENTS

A book is a story that has whispered its way through many hearts. Though I was lucky enough to be the one chosen to tell this story, I could not have done it without the help of many other eager hearts. Huge thank you to everyone who listened to me, encouraged me, got excited with me, looked after my daughter for me (my amazing parents), bought me coffee, all so that I could untangle the whispers and turn them into words. Words that became pages, then chapters, and finally a book. An especially big sea swept thank you to my brilliant and unstoppable agent, Claire Wilson. My ever patient and utterly glorious editor, Clare Whitston. And to all the team at OUP, who have shown so much enthusiasm and joy for Minnow and her shark's teeth. I am so lucky to have you.

Huge heartfelt thanks to the stunningly talented Sandra Dieckmann for cover art beyond my wildest mermaid dreams.

Extra special thanks to my parents, my friends, my family, and my beautiful sea-swimming daughter.

And of course, all the other gorgeous authors that I'm so happy to call my friends. You are like a sisterhood of brilliance swirling through the world of books . . .

And lastly for anyone who, like Minnow, has not yet found their place in the world, remember Arielka's advice: In the deepest dark, you must be the light.

Ready for more great stories?
Try one of these ...

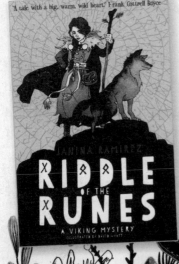

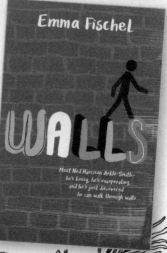